Write Off Line 2015

The Earth We Knew

Edited by
Jean Gilbert and Chad Dick

Tauranga Writers Publishing

www.taurangawriters.org.nz

This edition published in October 2015

ISBN   978-0-473-33935-7

Write Off Line 2015 contributors are Year 9 to 13 students of Avondale College, Cashmere High School, Gore High School, Hamilton Girls' High School, Katikati College, Marlborough Girls' College, Mt. Aspiring College, Mt. Maunganui College, New Plymouth Girls' High School, Northcote College, Rangi Ruru Girls' School, Rangitoto College, Sacred Hearts Girls' College Hamilton, St. Andrew's College, St. Mary's College, Tauranga Girls' College, Waimea College, Wakatipu High School, and Whakatane High School.

Original Cover Design by Kodi Murray

Write Off Line 2015

Contents

Foreword

Write Off Line 2015 continues the series through which Tauranga Writers aims to encourage and support young writers. We want to provide opportunities for secondary school students to not only practise their skills and receive feedback on their work, but also to become published authors. With this in mind, our annual writing competition allows us to bring together a collection of works that show the talent and imagination of the participants, and lets them experience the thrill of seeing their work in print.

For this, the fourth collection, we asked students to turn their imaginations towards science fiction, and focus on the theme of 'The Earth We Knew.' We received well over one hundred submissions from more than twenty different schools. In both poetry and prose, the students have surprised and delighted us, showing great skill in their use of words, and bringing humour, excitement, horror and fascination to the page. We wish we could have published more of the pieces, but sadly this was not possible. But all students received individual feedback, and we hope this encourages all to continue to write.

Running the Write Off Line competition involves considerable work and would not be possible without help. We are very grateful to Piper Mejia, who is the principal organizer of the event, and whose guidance has been invaluable. Lee Murray donated prizes, and we have also received support from SpecFicNZ with the running of the competition. We also thank our judges, Jan Goldie and Emma Shia, for their hard work in both decision making and providing feedback, and artist Kodi Murray for his magnificent and inspirational cover design.

Jean Gilbert and Chad Dick

CAITLIN DAVISON

The Earth We Once Knew

The Earth we once knew didn't contain weird things like
this.
There were no robots, aliens, or machines that go blitz.

We had to type on our phones, and drive on the ground.
Our prime minister wasn't a robot that bossed us around.

Flying cars now fill the sky,
and hover boards are way up high.

iPhone 20s are implanted in our brain,
and all we do is sit and complain.

We sit here acting all dreamy,
all our duties we shirk.
These days everyone is greedy,
while we put our machines to work.

Will we ever go back to how it was when cows still used to
moo?
Doesn't anyone even remember the Earth we once knew?

CAELEN KINLEY

Saving Earth in a Campervan

A man in dark sunglasses walked into the shady conference room. He did not take off his sunglasses. He scanned the room, gazing at the creatures sitting around the table. They all watched him as he sat down at their head.

"Welcome to the Licnuoc Council," he said. "As you know I am Lord of the Namuhs, from planet Htrae. I have called this meeting to speak to you about the most beautiful planet in the universe. The planet's inhabitants call it Earth. I am proposing that we drag this picturesque planet over to our orbit so we can admire it up close forever."

The members of the council looked at each other and shrugged.

The Lord of the Namuhs smiled. "So," he said, "I'll start immediately."

*

Jim Sandro knew that today would be a bad day. He groaned as he got off the cold hard floor of his bedroom. He wondered why he had slept on the floor instead of his nice bed. Then Jim remembered that he had been fired from his job as a car salesman the day before, because he had only sold one car in the last year. His boss had said that his performance had been appalling. The one car Jim had sold was to himself. He had left work, gone to a bar, got drunk, staggered home, and flopped onto the floor of his bedroom, missing the bed.

Someone knocked at his front door as Jim walked into the kitchen. The door burst open before he got there. His strange friend, Ordnas Mij, came running in, and barrelled straight into Jim's wiry body.

"Jim," gasped Ordnas, "you need to come with me now."

"Why?" asked Jim with confusion.

"Because the world is going to end in one minute!"

*

Jim groaned as he picked himself off another cold hard floor. He looked around in wonder; he was actually on a spaceship! After Ordnas had burst into his house, he had pulled Jim out the back door, and told him to get into the campervan that was sitting in the back yard. Then Ordnas had jumped into the campervan, pushed a button, and they started flying. The campervan produced a tremendous bang as it sped out of Earth's atmosphere and into outer space.

Ordnas came over carrying a glass of weird looking liquid, and gave it to Jim. "Drink up," said Ordnas. "This is a translator drink. It will help you to understand the alien's language. You will be able talk to them."

"Cool," said Jim as he gulped down the liquid. "So why am I here, and what happened to Earth?"

"Well," said Ordnas, "the leader of the Namuhs has dragged Earth over to his planet, and by doing that, he has destroyed all of civilisation. He did this because he thinks Earth is pretty. On that happy note, I need to stop to refuel my flying campervan at the next planet, Nrutas."

After Ordnas landed the flying campervan, he stepped out and told Jim to follow him to a bar.

Jim was still stunned at what had happened to Earth and, as he stepped down, he tripped and fell flat on his face. Jim groaned; this was the third time today he'd had to pick himself off a cold hard floor. He really needed a drink.

Jim walked over to the bar and said, "Two beers please."

The bartender looked down and Jim realised that he had five eyes: two on either side of his face, and one in the centre of his forehead. Jim screamed, bumping into Ordnas who grabbed him and shoved him into a booth, before sitting down himself.

"You can't just go round screaming at people," said Ordnas.

"Are you kidding?" shrieked Jim. "That guy had five eyes!"

"Yes," replied Ordnas. "And?"

"*And* that's not normal!"

"No," said Ordnas. "I have friends with 100 eyes, 30 arms and 55 noses."

"OH," gasped Jim feeling very faint. He looked out the window, and saw with horror that the campervan was flying away. "Uh, Ordnas, look at the campervan!"

Ordnas jumped straight through the window and pointed his keys at the campervan and pressed a button. The campervan flew down to settle next to Ordnas, who jumped into the campervan with a ray gun in his hand.

Jim heard a big Fizzoooooo!

Ordnas walked out holding a man with ten thousand eyes all over his body.

Ordnas pulled out an object that looked a bit like a phone and said, "Hello, I have a criminal for you."

In front of Jim's eyes the man disappeared with a pop!

"How did you do that?"

"Do what?" replied Ordnas as he rocketed the campervan out of Nrutas.

"How did you make that campervan-jacker disappear?"

"Oh," said Ordnas, "I handed him over to the police."

"Well, that makes perfect sense," said Jim.

"Good," smiled Ordnas, obviously not catching the sarcasm in Jim's voice.

"What are we going to do now?" exhaled Jim.

"Well," replied Ordnas, "we are going to go and steal back Earth."

*

Jim gazed out the window as the campervan whizzed along in space. He saw some weird things: a huge flying pig as big as a house, and green flying horses. But the weirdest thing was a large orange ship manned by green road cones, who were hopping around at the speed of a garden snail. Ordnas said that they had come from the Coney Way.

Finally, after what seemed like ages, Ordnas turned round in his driver's seat, and said in an ominous voice, "We're here."

Jim looked out the window in amazement. He couldn't comprehend what he was seeing. The planet Jim was looking at was five times bigger than Earth. He saw cars flying around - real cars like Lamborghinis, Ferraris and Porsches.

Ordnas landed the campervan on Htrae, and said, "We have to find a tow-truck, then we can pull Earth back to your solar system."

"Okay," said Jim. "And where do we find a tow-truck?"

"We go and buy one," Ordnas said as he walked towards a place that looked like a car dealership.

Soon Jim and Ordnas were zipping out of Htrae in their newly purchased tow-truck heading towards a much smaller planet, which Jim soon realised was Earth. Ordnas stopped and pressed a button. Jim heard a clunking sound, and looked back see a rusty old hook descend slowly towards the surface.

"That's not going to be able to pull Earth, is it?" said Jim. "Is it?"

Ordnas pushed another button and Jim heard the towline tension. Then Ordnas slammed down the accelerator, and the tow-truck zipped away from Htrae towing Earth behind it.

*

After they had put Earth back into its old orbit, they landed the tow-truck. Jim looked around. He saw that everything was overgrown. Only the plants and animals remained. All civilisation had been wiped off the face of the planet.

He gasped in horror. "This is not the Earth we knew…"

Blind

Cäcilie stared glassy-eyed at the teacher, who was attempting to engage his reluctant audience in the history lesson. The information had been drilled into them for years – the four world wars, the bombing of a continent, the dividing of Europe.

The teacher continued, "And when Europe split into two sectors after World War Four, those that tried to flee the country were blinded with UV light, and imprisoned in the Blind Camps of today."

Cäcilie had seen a Blind Camp once, when she was younger. She and her parents were walking a new track through the towering gorse bushes on the way home from her Grandpa's house. Her father had stopped so abruptly Cäcilie had run into him. Looking past her father she had seen a large grey building, surrounded by barbed wire. Behind the fence were people, thin, with hollow cheeks and ragged clothing.

"Briiiiiiing!"

At the piercing sound of the bell, Cäcilie jumped awake, and heaved her bag onto her shoulders, in a hurry to get to the auditorium for the monthly shots. Entering the auditorium, Cäcilie had only a short wait before a nurse approached and gave her the regular talk:

"This injection will slow your breathing rate down, allowing your body to cope with the air's high levels of CO_2. Any issues with your breathing, or odd symptoms, consult your doctor." As the needle went in, she felt the strange rush of chemicals beneath her skin. "All done," the nurse said, turning to the next student.

Cäcilie walked toward home alongside the empty road. Apart from the occasional bicycle, the roads were rarely used. Grandpa often told her stories of when the roads were wide and full of all kinds of vehicles, and the pavement was just a tiny sliver of concrete. This part of town depressed her; it was like a painting that had had all the colour sucked out of it, apart from the graffiti that covered many of the grey brick walls.

Cäcilie passed into the forest that crowded in on the town. The trees dwarfed her, reaching up into the sky with their healthy leaves and thick branches. At least *they* were benefitting from the deadly atmosphere. The smell of damp earth hung thick in the air. It was hard to imagine that without the help of the injection, the air would be toxic. Cäcilie let the silence and the peacefulness of the forest wash over her.

A rustle nearby broke the silence. There were no animals; only whirring insects that didn't need as much oxygen to survive. Shocked, she found the source of the noise on the ground, feeling in the dirt with his hands. The young boy raised his head.

"Hello?" he whispered breathlessly. His grey eyes stared straight ahead, unblinking and unmoving.

"You're a Blind," Cäcilie gasped. Her mind swirled. Should she turn him in? Help him?

"Please," he croaked desperately, tears streaming down his face. "Can I come with you?"

Cäcilie thought for a moment, but in her heart she already knew the answer.

"Follow me."

She could hear clumsy footsteps behind her as she walked, pausing sometimes to listen to where she was, and then continuing. Cäcilie jumped when the Blind grabbed her wrist. He apologised, but didn't let go.

"You were going too fast," he panted.

Cäcilie gave an inward shiver at the Blind's touch, and for the rest of the trip she remained extremely conscious of the hot hand on her wrist.

Once they were home, she hid him in the old shed and told him to stay quiet and to hide under a tarpaulin if someone came in.

"How will I know if it's you or someone else?" he asked.

She thought for a second. "I'll knock three times," she explained. Now that he was resting, his breathing had calmed. She wondered when his last injection was. "I'll bring you some food later," she said as she left. He looked like he needed it.

Later, Cäcilie lay awake, waiting for her parents to settle. She eased out of bed, retrieved a bowl of left-over soup from its hiding place, and slipped into the night.

"I thought you might have left me here," he said. "You took a long time."

"You're lucky I haven't told anyone about you," Cäcilie said defensively, placing the bowl in his outstretched hands. She started to apologise for the soup being cold, but he gulped it down.

"They don't feed us much at the Camps," the boy said.

Cäcilie felt suddenly guilty. She didn't even know the boy's name.

"So, what's your name?" she asked, sitting down next to him.

"Sentio," he said. "My mother told me it means something in Latin; I'm not sure what. She's gone now."

The next day Cäcilie biked out to see Grandpa. Afterwards, on the way home, she thought about what he had said. She had asked him what he thought about the Blinds. She had been scared that he would hate them, like everyone else seemed to. Grandpa had considered the question, and then replied that it was unfair that they had to pay the price for their ancestor's mistakes.

"The ones that roam free may be the ones that are truly blind," he had said. "Some people just can't accept that the Earth we knew is gone."

Cäcilie scavenged food from the kitchen that she knew her parents wouldn't miss. Sentio was still sitting on the tarpaulin, and opened his hands expectantly when she entered. She sat with him for much longer than yesterday, talking and laughing. Sentio told her stories of his friend Arlo's antics inside the Camp, and Cäcilie told him about life outside the Camp. Soon they fell into a friendly, peaceful silence.

"Um, can I touch your face? Please?" Sentio asked. He stared at Cäcilie with his glassy eyes, as if trying to judge her reaction, then reached up tentatively, and placed his palms on her cheeks, gently running his small, calloused hands over her face. "What colour is your hair?"

"Brown," she replied.

"And your eyes?"

"Blue."

He smiled at her. She smiled back, and wished that he could see it.

After dinner Cäcilie went to the bookshelf in the living room, and crouched down to the shelf where the language books and dictionaries were kept. She dislodged a thick Latin dictionary with a blue cover. Kneeling on the floorboards, she flicked through the book to find the definition: sentio – I feel.

The next morning Cäcilie went out to the shed before school. She knocked three times on the door, and then fished the key out of her pocket and went inside. She went cold.

Crouching down beside Sentio, she gave him a gentle nudge, and then placed a shaking hand on his neck. His skin was icy. A sob escaped her lips. She pulled him onto her lap and cradled his lifeless body, tears flowing down her cheeks and onto the tarpaulin. She cried until her throat was sore and her head was pounding.

"I feel," she whispered.

VIMALA VARGHESE

The Earth We Knew

The room was brightly lit when Tara walked in to start work. Beside her was the tiny new girl, Saffron. Multiple giant screens stood in every corner of the hall. In the centre was a giant stage on which stood a podium and the biggest screen in the room. Well-dressed men and women stood in groups around the room, hair styled immaculately, and holding flutes of champagne. Saffron and Tara rushed to the group of underdressed individuals who stood in the corner of the room, being surveyed by a woman wearing an eye-catching blue suit, and half-concealed evil look.

"Those are the rest of the proletarians. Us proletarians need to stick together at all costs. Understand?" Tara whispered urgently.

She sidled up to a tall, lanky boy wearing a faded sweatshirt, and old, torn pants.

"This is my friend, Kris," Tara said. The boy nodded, and smiled kindly. "Kris, this is Saffron. She's new." Tara eyed the stage. "So what's going on?"

"Pretty sure the big man right there wants us all dead," Kris whispered, nodding towards the stage. "Apparently they've designed a new video game where the proletarians are the avatars. You know, so they can make their little ones practise making us fight and kill each other."

The man in his seventies was standing behind the podium in a crisp black tuxedo, a sharp contrast against the white screen behind him. A bleached-blonde wig covered his balding head. His posture resembled the neck of an ostrich. The thin layer of sweat glistening on the makeup on his forehead became even more pronounced as his face suddenly filled the 80 inch hovering screens around the halls.

The man's voice droned,

"Ladies and Gentlemen, boys and girls... *The Earth We Knew* is the most creative and innovative idea our company, or any company, has created to date. This incredible virtual game will change the world of gaming *forever*. Now, thanks to Agon Gaming Industry, your sons and daughters can control *humans* in the virtual world. You heard that right! Agon have found a way to teleport proletarians into the *game itself*, and *your children* get to dictate their fates."

"Who is he?" Saffron whispered urgently, her knuckles whitening from clutching onto Tara.

"He's the boss man, Donald. The CEO, if you will," Tara said, keeping her eyes on the screen.

"What a funny name."

A small smile cracked though Kris' worried features. "Don't you go sayin' nothin' like that with the boss man around. He's the one who gets to decide if we get to live or die."

"He wouldn't just kill us like that, would he? That's against the law! We can fight back!" Saffron's pinched features grew more determined.

"There is no law, kiddo. The rich get to do whatever the rich want to do. *We* proletarians don't get to decide. Disobeying once cost my Momma her eye. I wouldn't try it if I were you," Tara whispered, her jaws set and expression grim.

On stage, Donald nodded slightly. A group of women in prim attire floated through the crowd, refilling champagne flutes, and smiling politely at the stiff and unsmiling guests.

"Now, as I was saying, *The Earth We Knew* is a revolutionary game set over 100 years ago in a time when humans harvested oxygen from trees and kept animals in their households. The main objective is for the test subjects to find their way around this wild and unruly world, where the roads were inhabited by machines called cars and buses, and airspace was only used by aeroplanes. Our group of skilled scientists have created genetically modified beings, or monsters, that each subject will have to fight at the end of every level, in order to advance to the next. All decisions made by the subjects will be dictated by *your* sons and daughters!

"Your children are the future leaders of this planet. It is vital that they acquire the skill to control and dictate to proletarians. *The Earth We Knew* will teach our children to refine and master problem solving, critical thinking, and administrating the lower classes. So, this being the case, let us thank our wonderful sponsors who have made this all possible."

"What a load of rub…" started Tara, only to be interrupted by a slender body crashing into her.

"Oh! I'm so terribly sorry!"

A head of curly blonde hair clouded Tara's vision as the girl frantically stood up. Tara's eyes adjusted enough to see the Upper Class lapel pin that was attached to the girl's tight-fitting ball gown.

Tara's eyes narrowed as she hugged Saffron closer to her body. "What do you want?"

"I'm so sorry to bother you, but I was doing a class project and…" the girl's voice trailed off as her eyes landed on Kris and Saffron.

"What are you looking at?" growled Kris.

"I'm so sorry, but I've just never seen so many brown kids together in real life before!" Her eyes were wide and earnest.

Tara's jaw set.

"Well, now you have. What do you want?"

The girl blinked twice, and then smiled, undeterred.

"Well, I was just doing a class project where we have to interview a minority to see how they plan to survive *The Earth We Knew*, and…"

"Monica! What are you doing, making conversation with proletarians?" a woman cried out in fury, rushing to drag the girl away from the trio.

The rest of the commoners around them looked on curiously as the mother dragged the girl off towards a group of guests.

"It was for a school project, Mum," Monica whispered loudly. To Tara, she called out over her shoulder, "Hey, don't listen to what these people are saying. I'll try my best to make sure you three will stay alive during the game, ok?"

"Monica, I've told you before, you talk to this kind for too long, and you start catching their infections," the mother furiously hurled at her daughter.

Tara sighed, and turned to Saffron, whose eyes were welling up.

"We're really going to die aren't we?" Saffron whimpered.

"Hey, we're going to try our best to stay alive. Even if we die in the game, they won't actually kill us. Our bodies will be revived, and delivered to our families. At the end of the day, this is what we're paid to do. Remember what matters most is that the money we make goes back to our families. We're helping them survive, ok?"

"Tara, you're lying…"

"Proletarians!" a shrill voice cut through the crowd. A woman dressed in a black suit and skirt walked up to them. A deadly smile adorned her face. "Who's ready to go first? The children are ready, at their playing stations and now it's your time to go in!"

Her smile grew wider, and more strained. Her lips stretched over her pearly white teeth as her cheeks twitched.

"The adventure awaits you! Let *The Earth We Knew* begin!"

When We Return

Seven shining aspects of Earth's surface hovered in space. Originally they had been untouched and priceless. Now they were scarred and worthless. Searlie shook her flat head. Her long waterfall of what seemed to be pale peach hair, reaching from the top of her scalp to her waist, floated and swayed in the air. Disappointed, she turned away from the viewing platform. The solar-plate closed behind her with a hiss, blocking out the ghastly sight.

They had come back expecting to find Earth's pristine surface lush and green with life, flourishing in the perfect atmosphere, and growing conditions created by The Ones. Instead, it was dull and polluted, full of a species' waste and filth. Only a tiny portion of Earth's great bounty of life remained, and that tiny morsel was steadily being eaten up by greed and money.

No one had been expecting the situation to be so bad. All that beautiful art shattered by one careless creation. One animal to which someone had foolishly added a little too much intelligence, a little too much curiosity, and suddenly everything was ruined. Billions of years of work wasted in just one moment. The news that she brought to the council would not be good.

Her long tangles swished slightly as they propelled her along the shimmering corridor. The multiple extended membranes branched out from what humans would have likened to feet, and allowed her to stick to almost any surface. Thinner, more delicate ones laced out from her hands. Six more branched out from underneath flowing layers of a substance similar to silk just above her shoulders. She could control her hand-tangles with careful precision to manipulate the most delicate of crafting tools, a crucial feature of her race.

Her entire body had faded to a flaccid grey showing her disappointment. The only exceptions were her seven eyes, one in her forehead, and one in each of her six hands. They were a pale aqua with tints of green and glowed slightly in the light of deep-space, reflecting back a hidden light. Her *thrin*, or partner, had lavender eyes that contained hidden flecks of gold that came out whenever he was happy, or surprised, giving him his name: Selonar, or hidden sun.

She broke out of her reverie in time to see one of the council floating towards her. His colours swirled, a mix of sick yellow and pale green, broadcasting his discomfort and unease about their current situation. Behind him scurried a group of *nenyon*, assistants, who were frantically trying to collect his various pods of info-stacks, and sort them into organised piles of notes, which could then be stored in the data box floating behind them. At the sight of Searlie, the council member stopped in mid-stride, and suppressed his emotions so that his colours shifted to a neutral blue. He touched his sixth and seventh hand tangles with her in greeting before stepping back to regard her carefully.

"Have you seen it?" he asked her, lowering his voice so that the *nenyon* behind could not hear.

At Searlie's nod, he sadly shook his head, and turned three of his hand-eyes away in shame.

"Such a waste of our country's most beautiful art. We must try to save what little of it we can, how ever we can."

Searlie nodded sadly, and couldn't help but feel regret that everything had gone so horribly wrong. Her colours changed to a swirl of pale pink and gold in sympathy. She quickened her tangles in order to get to the council in time.

*

Silence descended as The Prime stepped forward. The main council member controlled all debates. His word was final, no matter how close the votes were. His extended memory meant he could recall previous documents and agreements long forgotten by everyone else. Most of their history was stored in his mind. The council had been discussing the issue of the human race for the last *minth* – approximately one hour of Earth time – and they still had not decided what they should do. Some screamed for deletion. Others called for them to be moved to another planet with all their toxic waste and refuse.

Searlie glanced over to Selonar, and saw him lost deep in thought, his colours muted and dull. Personally, Searlie thought they should just leave the humans to their own destruction, and begin again on a new planet. Eventually humankind would discover that the Earth's resources were finite and the people must begin to protect what little they had left. She could begin her arts again to create a new species for a new planet, hopefully one that was not too intelligent, and then carefully sculpt it over the years to achieve her desired effect. It would be too much bother to move an entire species and their junk to a new place. The other intergalactic councils may not be willing to help them correct a mistake they did not make. She sighed heavily, and let her gaze wander around the room again.

The Prime paused for a moment, waiting for silence to fall, before he lifted his great voice to the room. "We are here to discuss the issue of the human race, and the Earth we knew. What we decide today will determine our futures tomorrow. We have heard several suggestions about what we must do, and now we must come to an agreement."

A small ripple of murmurs spread throughout the room, before complete silence fell again.

The Prime continued. "Several ideas have been put forward. We must choose the path we think best, not just for us, but for our whole system. Eventually these creatures will learn how to fly, and the day may come when they will reach our own home planet. We must make a decision before they spread too far. So, we vote."

Reverently, everyone bowed their heads, and linked their first and second tangles with their *thrin*. Slowly at first, then with increasing speed, small flecks of light spun away from the pairs and flowed towards The Prime. The room became filled with spinning points of light, all streaking up towards a central focal point. There was a long moment of silence filled with shifting colours and shades as everyone wondered what choice had been made.

The Prime opened his eyes, and lifted his tangles to speak. There was a small pause, with the only noise the ship singing slightly in deep-space. All sound stopped as everyone waited to hear what the fate of the human race would be.

DARIA BEATTIE JOHNSON

Dying Stars

We sit, silent beneath dying stars,
gazing upon the landscape's scars.
As dust and smog devour the air,
the putrid stench of guilt and fear
crawls beneath the human skin
to fester and infect the next of kin.

The burning flesh of long lost souls
is harvested, and used for coals.
The haunting wail of an infant's cry
echoes under a desolate sky,
never to be cradled or held again,
only destined for a life of pain.

No screech of tyres or city lights
only spirits roam in cold, dead nights.
Buildings crumble, burn, decay,
humanity's pride stands in dismay,
abandoned, derelict, lonesome and bare,
riddled with horror, disease and despair.

Tales of children smothered at birth
by mothers gone mad, eyes lit with mirth.
Ghosts of those whose memory wanes
who've lost the pump of blood in their veins,
and those who do recall, spend their hours
dreaming of a long lost world once ours.

So, we sit, silent beneath dying stars,
gazing upon the landscape's scars,
and we ponder, wonder, reflect
we, torn asunder by the pain of regret.

Yet a promise hangs, to start anew,
and, a whisper, just a whisper,
of the Earth we knew.

MAX HALL

Change

A world in trouble for mistakes we made
no turning back or chance to save.
A thought of change yet nothing is done,
so we read and we write, we walk and we run.

We stay in our boxes, lonely with confusion,
dream of a chance to make a revolution,
but all this deep thought is simply delusion,
and the hope we once had is merely illusion.

The Earth we knew when life was first seeded,
when the world lived in peace, and only took what it
needed.

Did we know of a time where life didn't cost?
Sadly what was and once dreamed is lost.
Do we see the chances we didn't take?
We've got a life to live, decisions to make.

Will we finally know of this fate we have set?
When the end comes, nothing's worse than regret.

So step out of this box and make this your day;
There's a world of choice so get on your way.
In fifty years' time when we finally know,
we'll wish we started fifty years ago.

Now is the time, there's no better than here,
let's make this right and call it square.
We still have time to re-arrange;
to make the world better only starts with a

CHANGE.

LAURIE DUNCAN

The Lurking Shadow

Silence,
Slicing through the elapsed city,
An unwelcome host from
The Earth we knew.

Collapsed, cracked,
Crushed, crippled,
Tangled irons providing
No safe haven.

I whispered to you
Unaware of the hidden eyes
Peeking out and
Watching us in the twilight.

It came out at us
Cloaked and Disguised
Like a ghost,
A shadow in this secluded place.

Silence,
Slicing through the elapsed city,
An unwelcome host from
The Earth we knew.

AMBER KELSO

Lost in Translation, I Think

Recorder's Note: There are a few words missing here and there, and honestly, the scribe that wrote all this down for me is useless on his best days. The words were just lost in translation, I think. Although, most of them seem to be all the expletives and insults everyone used. Nepthys has a tendency to omit anything he doesn't deem proper. The constant interruptions probably didn't help either...

I've always loved the sound of the rain. When the wind is wild, it charges in waves, rolling the water over everything. I haven't been in the rain for a good long while. Then again, no one has. All the water we have is scattered throughout the fragile ecosystem we've built in the ruins of this thing people call "civilization." Well, I didn't help build it. I just sort of crashed through their "indestructible" roof, and landed in it. I managed to set off every single alarm in the place while I was at it. Nepthys was *not* happy. At all.

-HOW MANY TIMES DO I HAVE TO [omitted] TELL YOU, ZEKE? MY NAME IS NOT NEPTHYS, YOU [omitted]!

-CALM DOWN, OLD MAN! IT'S A FORCE OF HABIT, ALRIGHT?

There's no privacy in this place.

Man, I tell you, this dimension's version of Nepthys can *cuss*. He swears like a sailor at the smallest things. It's absolutely hilarious watching Drew's face turn so many shades of red when Nep gets going.

Anyway, I'm going on a tangent.

So this version of reality consists of a lovely planet, Earth, absolutely mauled by humanity and their egotistical lack of

26

foresight. They realised a little too late that pieces of paper and lumps of rock can't physically help them survive. The big fat cats died real quick. All those paranoid [omitted] with the bunkers and the survivalists disappeared without so much as a *"we told you so."* Everyone left reckons they were killed off, or that they can't be bothered with the idiots that have supposedly inherited the Earth.

Pleeaase!

The only reason they've lived this long is because of Drew and me. Their filtration system was pathetically antiquated, and as for their 'defence system,' five RPGs, four assault rifles, three flamethrowers, two nukes, and a handful of IEDs do not an arsenal make. That makes for a fun round of paint-ball. Not an apocalypse-worthy weapons stash.

Trying to convince them of this, however, was about as hard as explaining our existence to Drew: unpleasant, difficult, and just damn painful. Nepthys – sorry, I keep forgetting his name is Farrens here – and the rest of these bloody cultists are still convinced that everything outside their little bunker/lab/city-thing hasn't gone to [omitted]. His opinions were, and still are, too ingrained: "We have everything we need to restore order. The ramifications of the event were clearly overestimated…"

"[omitted], man, have you actually stepped *outside?*"

"We have observed local surroundings. Recent contact from existing resistance groups confirms that all resources remain intact, ready for retrieval and re-use."

"Oh, you mean the footage that I have pointed out *more than once*, is a feedback loop from 10 [omitted] years ago? As are the audio clips you supposedly 'receive'," (at this point I was so frustrated I almost hit him in the face with my sarcastic quote-unquote gestures) "from *resistance groups!* There's nothing to [omitted] resist out there! The Earth we knew is gone, Farrens! Long gone! Every day you [omitted] sit here petting your plants, and waiting for some [omitted] sign from above is another day you've wasted instead of [omitted] helping yourselves get out of this [omitted]!"

As you can probably tell, at this point I was ranting so much I didn't even breathe. Oh, I can do that by the way. Not breathe. A handy side-effect of being composed entirely of dark matter. Which in turn is what lets me slip between dimensions (*cough, layers of matter, cough*) at extremely inconvenient and annoying moments.

Anyway, so I was just about ready to quit and walk out with their 'weapons stash,' when something ironic happened. Their communications were hijacked.

Well, everything was hijacked.

By *me.*

Or rather, a 'projection' of me. A small bit of myself that didn't end up quite where it should have when I turned up in this dimension. Instead of being in my head where I can keep an eye on it, little pieces like this one have a tendency to say: "Nope, not doing this [omitted] anymore, bye!" and go off to do their own thing. And I get to clean up after them. Or rather, myself. It makes for a bit of a headache.

This splinter of myself had decided to have a bit of a play with the cultists' old weapons systems. And here I was wondering where my destructive and violent tendencies had gone.

-THERE THEY ARE!

-FOR CRYING OUT LOUD, DREW! I'M TRYING TO RECORD HERE! AND YOU WERE [omitted] THERE. YOU KNOW THAT I RE-ASSIMILATED THAT PART OF ME EVENTUALLY! I REALLY WON'T HESITATE TO-[extended period of omitted text] – AND GUT YOU NOW! JEEZ. WHAT DOES IT TAKE FOR SOME PRIVACY AROUND HERE?

So my more destructive tendencies –

-YOU MEAN YOU ON A NORMAL DAY?

-SHUT UP, DREW!

– decided to push all those big red buttons you're really not supposed to touch, and launched every single weapon squirreled away – including the nukes – straight at us.

So real quick-like, Drew and I pulled off our gloves (quite literally), shoes, jackets, and pants… We exposed as much of our skin as was socially acceptable, OKAY?! And tried to touch as many other people as possible.

Both of us being made of dark matter, we can redirect massive amounts of energy towards ourselves instead of others with no adverse effects. We're like the universe's ultimate version of cockroaches! Unfortunately, it requires us to be close to the atoms we want to protect. In your face close. Skin on skin is even better. So we grabbed onto as many people as possible on an atomic level… And then everything hit us.

Recorder's Note: Man, I'm sorry guys. You missed out on half the story. I really need to supervise Nep when he writes this stuff down. Half of what he omitted wasn't even swearing, insults, or threats of mild bodily discomfort. This guy's no fun. I need a new scribe…

The Houston Toad

His neighbour was staring at him again.

What was his name? Mr McDaniels? Mr McGilly?

He was an Ideal, it was obvious. His skin was creamy under the wrinkles and deepening frown lines where his eyebrows had a nasty habit of knitting together. It wove across his frail bones like the delicate stitches of a tapestry. Not a mark or blemish breached the surface. His eyes, smooth as washed pebbles, sat in exact alignment with one another. Yet no amount of perfection could hide the ice settling beneath them. They followed Bishop over the fence as he walked down to the letter box, his hand never stopping its task of swivelling the hose nozzle back and forth over the petunias.

Every morning, at exactly seven o'clock, Mr McGilly went out into his garden, and watered his petunias. And every morning, as Bishop collected his mail, his neighbour would scowl at him. It had become a routine with them, their own little greeting. Bishop didn't take it too personally. Mr McGilly scowled at everyone. But there was a very special scowl he reserved just for him. A scowl that said Mr McGilly was looking at something very wrong, something very wrong indeed. Something that shouldn't be there.

Bishop rummaged through his mail. A few bills, magazine subscriptions, a letter from the council that very politely asked him to report to the Sector Six Police Department to renew his citizenship. He pocketed the mail, dodging Mr McGilly's beady little eyes and the others glancing out of the identical dollhouses stretching as far as the eye could see.

The grass was all the same length. The hedges were all trimmed the same way. The letterboxes were all identical, like handsome

30

soldiers standing to attention. They were as plain and boring as the people who lived in them.

Bishop glanced back at Mr McGilly's petunias swaying under the early morning light. They were like the people really. All perfect. All the same. All united.

All except him.

Eden prided itself on being a close-knit community, but their closeness didn't quite extend as far as Harry Bishop. A Defect anywhere other than Sector One was a rare find, like a Houston Toad.

And no one liked Houston Toads.

It hadn't always been like this, Bishop reminded himself, although as the days passed, those six words drifted further and further away, like a dream you couldn't quite remember.

Time was everyone was a Defect, though they hadn't known it, obviously. But then they cracked it. The Perfection Code. That's what the scientists called it. Complete manipulation of the genes inside a human embryo. You could have it all – beauty, strength, intelligence. Perfect puzzle pieces stitched together to make every human on the planet.

Every human who could afford it, that is.

Bishop had to be one of the only human beings living in Sector Nine who hadn't been born in a test tube. Defects were bundled away into Sector One, and banned from any other sectors, unless they had special citizenship issued by the courts. It was out of courtesy to the Ideal population, they had said. Bishop could understand that. Spend generation upon generation surrounded by perfection, and anything less becomes almost… a monster.

So, that was the end of the line for the Defects. After all, we wouldn't want any reminders of the world we knew, now, would we? They were hidden away in Sector One like skeletons in the closet.

Except him.

The squeal of tires snapped him out of his thoughts. Up ahead, someone was running. No one ran in Eden. They barely even walked briskly. As he got closer, Bishop could make out the plump face of a kid. He couldn't have been older than seventeen, cheeks red and swollen like two giant plums. His eyes bulged in their sockets, not the bright, sparkling eyes Bishops saw every day. Dull, granite eyes.

Defect.

He pelted past Bishop,

"Hey," Bishop called out. He didn't look back. "Hey!"

A black van tore down the road, hot on the boy's heels. Bishop ran after him, digging around in his jacket for his police badge.

The kid rounded a corner. The van screamed to a halt. Bishop dug his heels into the pavement, almost crashing into the bonnet.

A bald man with a pierced face and a number of angry-looking tattoos jumped out, and tackled the kid to the ground.

"You like that, huh?" he snarled, kicking the kid in the shin, hauling him to his feet.

"For Pete's sake, Riff, go easy on him, would you?" Bishop said. "He's just a kid."

Riff spun on his heel to face him, and leered. He rolled his tongue over his lip, gave a little bow.

"Evening, Officer," Riff said, tipping an imaginary hat. "Don't mind me, just taking out the trash."

Riff was a smuggler, part of a group of lowlifes the Council hired to catch Defects trying to sneak into the Sectors. They were all Ideals, but that was about where their strengths ended.

Riff rammed the kid into the side of the van. Tears streamed down the kid's face as he choked into the cool metal. A few Ideals peeked through the cracks in their curtains. No one came outside.

Bishop took a step forward. "Let go of him."

Riff waggled a finger. "Ah-ah-ah. Kid's got no I.D., which means he's here illegally, making it my sworn duty to bring him in. Speaking of which..." He gave Bishop a quick once over. "You've got yours, I assume?"

Bishop fixed him with a glare, and dug into his pocket as the kid squirmed helplessly. Defects were required by law to show proof of their citizenship when asked, no matter their rank, otherwise they were open to arrest, or detainment.

He flashed his I.D.

Riff's smile faded a little.

"Everything seems to be in order," he said begrudgingly. "Expires in a few days. You should get that fixed. Could cause all sorts of trouble."

"I'll keep that in mind," Bishop murmured.

Riff barrelled past him, and shoved the kid into the back of the van. In the driver's seat, Riff gave Bishop one last wave as he took off screaming around the corner.

Bishop looked back at the dollhouses, trying to shake from his mind what the kid was in for, trapped in the Defect detention cells at the Smuggler's base. It was not like Bishop could have done anything, even if he'd wanted to. Justice didn't come to Defects easily.

He wove his way back through the dollhouses. Plastic people peeked out, watching as the Houston Toad drifted past the dancing petunias all in a line. As he disappeared into his house, Bishop knew that they all silently hoped that, this time, he wouldn't come back out.

What Once was Ours

I'm running. Running very fast. There's no time to lose. The professor's gone mad. Well, he's *officially* gone mad. He was *actually* bonkers a few years ago.

I'm running straight towards his lab. I'm running *towards* his lab. Maybe I'm bonkers too. That's fine.

I skid around a corner and try not to bump into the hover-chairs that plague the corridors. Ever since the world's greatest minds figured out how to make things hover, *they* went bonkers with *everything*. So, everyone's gone bonkers. Brilliant.

A pair of scientists are racing my way, worried looks lining their features. As soon as I race into view, they look relieved.

"Mister Jones!" they call to me.

"Uncle Holst?" I ask.

"Yes. How did you…"

"He called me."

"Oh?"

"He wants to talk to me."

"He's cracked."

"I know." I push past them and suddenly stop. "Oh, and guys?"

"Yes, Mister Jones?"

"Call me Jonesy," I say, flashing them a brief smile.

Then I turn and sprint along the now-deserted corridor. I'm sure those two are the last from up the tower. I head towards the elevator, but the ground shakes, as lightning flashes and thunder rumbles, and it begins to rain.

"Uncle Holst," I moan, dismissing the elevator idea entirely. "What did you do?"

It takes a good six and a half minutes to reach the top of the tower by the stairs. I'm panting by the end, but I have a feeling that the world is going to end. And that my uncle is going to end it. The nutcase.

I reach the door to his quarters. I place my palm on the security pad next to the door. It slides open like those doors from *Star Trek*. It always baffled me how Uncle Holst trusts me to come and go as I please in his quarters with all of his delicate equipment. I run through the open door into the dark room, and hang a left. I know my way around here with my eyes closed. There is a strategically placed wardrobe less than two metres from the door, so if anyone breaks in in the dark, they crash straight into the wardrobe, and wake Uncle Holst. And then they get shot with some sort of ray gun.

His ray guns are weird. I was playing with one when I was four, and it turned my skin magenta for a few days. Uncle Holst said that I was lucky I didn't grab the one that turned people inside out.

I race from the dark maze and into the bright lights of his living quarters. I don't stop there. Uncle Holst will be in his laboratory. He's always in his laboratory. The door to his lab is at the other end of this corridor. It's propped open as it always is when he's expecting me. I skid to a halt on the smooth marble floor stopping a foot away from my uncle.

His back is turned to me, so I get a full view of the back of his head. His greying blond hair surrounds his head in an Albert-Einstein-esk halo. His pristine white lab coat hangs down and gathers around his shins. He is staring at the holo-screens in front of him, each covered in numbers and equations.

"Uncle Holst?" I ask, reaching out to put a hand on his shoulder.

He turns to me before I can, his green eyes flashing with the light of youth despite the creases lining his face.

"Jonesy, m'lad! Glad you're here! I saw you took the stairs. Good idea," he says, an encouraging smile on his face. I smile back briefly.

"Uncle Holst, what's going on?"

Uncle Holst laughs. "Jonesy, you're old enough to call me by my first name, you know!"

I sigh. He does this every time. "Fine. Uncle Duncan, what's going on?" I repeat.

His first name is Duncan, but I have called him 'Uncle Holst' since – well – since I could speak.

Uncle Duncan laughs again. "I'm going to change the world!" he declares, throwing his arms out as if to hug the whole world.

"How? And why?" I ask, the gears in my brain working overtime.

"How? Well, m'lad, it's simple! I have created a device that will strike those with greed and darkness in their minds with lightning; a special lightning, mind you, that will incinerate them completely on the spot! All evil, petty crimes, and mad tyrants will be gone in one *zap!*" he cries, waving his arms to accentuate his point. "Those who are good in their hearts will not be harmed at all!"

I'm trying to process this. Slowly. *"How?!"* I demand.

"Through a brilliant mix of science, technology, psychology, theology and philosophy!" he informs me brightly.

"Why?" I ask.

Uncle Duncan eyes me.

"What on Earth do you mean, m'lad?" he asks.

"You're going to kill what'll be probably over half of the human race!"

Uncle Duncan shrugs. "If that's what it takes to cleanse the Earth of their mark, then yes."

"Wouldn't what you're doing classify yourself as a 'bad person?'" I reason.

Maybe seeing that he's possibly placing himself in danger might bring him out of this… delusion.

To my dismay, he shrugs again. "If I'm a bad person, then I too should be cleansed off this Earth."

"What if it was me, or Laura?" I ask frantically.

Laura is my little sister, and Uncle Duncan has been caring for us for seventeen years, since our mother and father died.

Uncle Duncan's shoulders sag. "Then you would be unfit to live upon this beautiful planet," he says, simply.

"Shouldn't you consult the authorities first?"

"They would only stop me."

"Me too."

Uncle Duncan reaches out and ruffles my unruly black hair. "Why, m'lad? It's for the greater good of the planet!"

"If you want to do good for the planet, you'd want to get rid of buildings and houses and plant some trees! You'd want to purify lakes and clean up oceans! Save rare creatures! Not wiping out… the ones who ruined… all that…" I trail off.

I see what Uncle Duncan means now. It's to stop mankind from continuing to pillage like we do. To return to the Earth we knew.

"Do I have your permission?" Uncle Duncan asks suddenly, surprising me.

His green eyes study my face intensely, trying to divine my emotions.

"Why do you need my permission?" I ask.

He chuckles.

"It's polite, no?"

I take a deep breath. "I'm bonkers," I mutter.

Uncle Duncan chuckles. I sigh. I close my eyes, and open them. I hug my uncle.

"I might not live through this," he warns me.

I nod slowly. I close my eyes again.

"I'm not watching. Go for it."

I hear him sigh, then a click. And a sizzle. I open my eyes. Uncle Duncan is gone. I sigh. He's bonkers. I'm bonkers. We're all bonkers.

A Bad Day in Hell

Deep in the fiery pits of Hell, a horned creature sat on his comfortable armchair — literal *arm*chair — with one hand holding a cup of boiling tea and the other carrying a book. The warm fire, placed next to his bookshelf, blazed with flames the colours of the sun. He eagerly opened to the first page and tranquillity cascaded over him as his mind settled in the new fantasy. His black eyes scanned the page before a loud *thump* caused him to look upwards.

A teenage girl had fallen through his roof, and was sprawled out on the floor.

"For Lord's sake, Asterah, I thought you fixed the leak!" he yelled in annoyance to his wife.

"I thought you fixed it, Lucifer!" Asterah replied in a distant voice from another room. "I thought you'd be grateful for these humans! Imagine what you can do with their blood!"

"It's not a good thing when they fall down here every minute!"

Sighing, Lucifer placed his bookmark in the second page, and slowly stood up. He walked towards the unconscious girl, and dragged her by her arms out of the living room and down the hallway, dropping her in a room with a few other unconscious humans.

"Imbecilic humans always managing to find these portals," he muttered under his breath.

He walked in haste back to his comfortable armchair, hoping his tea was still hot. It was, he confirmed after bringing it to his lips and sipping the warm liquid. Picking up his book, he resettled. The words formed pleasant pictures in his head: there was a ship rocking violently from side to side on dangerous waves, a sailor falling from the side of the ship, his shipmates yelling for help. However, another loud bang disintegrated the image in his mind.

"Dear Fiery Furnace, don't tell me it's another one..." Lucifer murmured.

He braced himself as he glanced at the floor in front of him.

It was a young adult man.

"Give me a break, you foolish humans! All I am asking for is a break!" he yelled as he slapped his book on a table, before dragging the man out of the room. As he passed his wife's room, she glanced up at him.

"Ah, we really do need to fix the hole," she observed.

"Yes, thank you for the *wonderful* advice, Asterah," he replied, then added, "And I thought any creature from the Earth we *knew* was stupid enough."

He hissed several similar comments of anger before he was back in the armchair with his book in his hand. His throat itched for warmth, and so he brought the tea to his lips, and poured a little into his mouth. It was cold. Lucifer forced the cup down onto the table beside him, spilling drops of tea onto his open book in the process.

"You've got to be kidding me! I've got tea on the book, and I only bought it yesterday," he gasped in disbelief.

He was about to snatch his book and attempt to read for the third time, but his wife walked into the room.

He sighed. "Yes, dear, what is it you want?"

"Well, Lucifer, turns out there must be another hole in the portal."

"Why do you say that, Asterah?"

"Another creature from Earth fell through the roof of the bathroom."

He opened his mouth to yell a profanity, but thought better of it. Following Asterah into the bathroom, he almost lost his temper at what he saw.

There, before his very eyes, was a squealing pig stuck in the bowl of the toilet.

"That's it; I'm quitting this job."

JUSTINE LIM-RANOLA

The Past's Remains

Our Earth was never lush,
Nor was it ever green,
Mountains of carcass,
Seas of decaying fins.

We were left with the remains
Of the generations past,
Artificial living
They knew wouldn't last.

We were the results of
A miscalculation,
That we could survive off
Broken innovations.

We became the prisoners
Of the place we called home,
Cages made of demise,
Bars of ivory bone.

Our ancestors left us
In a never-ending maze,
Where our only option was
To go up into space.

So we packed up the last
Of our humanity,
And went off on our journey,
Full of uncertainty.

Up among the twinkling darkness,
Realising from the view,
We were the generation
That the Earth never knew.

NIAMH COOPER

The Earth We Once Knew

The Earth we once knew standing
alone in the vast unknown,

The Earth we once knew, no longer
full of vast luscious lands
and working hands.

Rather, all that still stands are dark
lonesome nuclear waste lands.

So far away stands the Earth we once
knew,

The one we were gifted.

Although very few knew of the true
beauty that it held,

The roaring blue oceans and the
crisp green grass.

Ruled by a queen,
the damage we were causing
was unseen.

The Earth we once knew began to die,
but we were still hung up on the
things we could buy.

The Earth we once knew, the one we were gifted, now
standing alone in the
vast unknown with no one to call it
home,
And
The home we now know, although it
has many to call it home,
has no home to give.

JAYNIE YANG

The Sun Auction

January 20th 4529

"**Number 45 at one hundred and thirty seven million; I repeat, one hundred and thirty seven million. How about one hundred and thirty eight million, eh? I'm at one hundred...**" The auctioneer's voice fades into a steady rhythm. A number flashes onto the hologram behind the auctioneer signalling a new bid.

"**Number 25 at one hundred and thirty eight million; I repeat...**"

I'm sitting next to the window of the space ship, one hand on the glass. I can feel the warmth of the sun, a bright flaming beacon that calls to me, desperately asking for help. It's surrounded by satellites, millions and millions seeking solar power, blocking its rays from reaching the planets. Everyone in this room is able to make a bid, but more than half are scientists, hired by rich buyers to assess the condition of this particular sun lot.

A young woman sits in the seat next to mine, and places her hand onto the window, sighing when it touches.

"It's a shame that we don't get to feel this on Earth," she says, running her hand over the smooth glass of the window. "The heat feels really nice. Maybe Earth wouldn't be so bleak if there was a little sunshine."

I nod in agreement. Everyone relies on electricity for lighting on Earth because the sun's rays are being blocked by massive solar-panelled satellites owned by various important figures. Even now an auction is taking place to sell a section of the sun; a rare opportunity, as next to no one would give up free power. No one feels the warmth of a ray of sunshine on their face anymore. The next generation will probably never even know light from the sun.

"What would you do if you had a lot?" I ask her.

She pauses, and mulls over my question. After a few seconds, she says, "I wouldn't use it to harness power. Instead, I would leave it so the people at least could receive a little bit of sunshine. I'm currently researching how plants can be revived. And you?"

"I would do the same. Everybody deserves to know the warmth of a ray of sunshine."

The auctioneer's booming voice rings out across the room.

"Number 12 at one hundred and fifty one million; I repeat, Number 12 at one hundred and fifty one million. Can I get one hundred and fifty two million? I repeat…"

"I used to research exo-planets for any signs of life for a wealthy client."

"Why?" she asks, youthful face wrinkled in confusion. "It's been confirmed that making contact with other life forms is a big risk."

It has hardly been ten minutes, and she is already beginning to grow on me. Perhaps it's the inquisitiveness that reminds me of myself in my younger years, or the innocent air she possesses.

"Number 25 has raised it to one hundred and fifty two million. I repeat…"

"It was quite a while ago. About 14 years in fact…"

Four others and I were hired, fresh out of university, by a wealthy stockholder of a large business. We were assigned to find planets with suitable living conditions on the pretext of finding new life. At the start I honestly thought I was searching for life outside Earth. But gradually, when our client started rushing us, we realised the truth. By then it was too late. We had already found three different planets that could support human life. I suppose it was obvious from the start. Why would a drone on a mission to find extra-terrestrial life need to be equipped with missiles and nuclear bombs?

Our client was looking for a planet to inhabit and make his own. Another Earth. That was a concept I hadn't been able to understand at the time because why would you need another Earth? Surely, our Earth wasn't so bad? He asked my colleagues and me if we wanted to go; three of us including myself declined, but the other two took the offer.

"Number 84 at one hundred and fifty three million. I repeat..."

"Why didn't you go?" she asks, eyes bright with curiosity.

I throw a glance at my client who is hunched over his seat clutching something in his quivering hands. I recognise it as an ancient relic that people used in the early 3000s, a utensil that eventually died out when food became easily-chewable freeze-dried cubes and bottled liquefied mush. It was known as a 'fork.' He keeps it around his neck on a chain, and refers to it as his lucky charm, one that has been passed down for generations in his family.

"The reason nobody wants to invest anything into saving this planet is because it costs too much money with next to no gain. The reasoning is simple: why should I waste so much on this when I can leave and invest elsewhere?" I say. She smiles faintly as I talk to her. "It was then that I realised, even if you move to another planet, the inevitable will keep happening over and over again. No one, including myself, is doing anything to change. The Earth we knew is on the brink of extinction. Now that technology has been refined, we will no longer go through stages such as farming, but instead go straight to building factories and sky scrapers. The planet will be polluted, and when that happens, we will move again to another planet. Soon, we will be star hopping, leaving behind a trail of abandoned, barren planets."

At these words, she sucked in a sharp breath.

"Is there any hope that this might not happen? That it can be changed?" she asks, face pinched with worry.

"Number 25 at one hundred and fifty five million. I repeat..."

I smile, a smile I didn't think I had, one that makes the corner of my eyes wrinkle. I smile because she dared to find an answer to the question present in every single one of us.

"There is always hope."

My client's number flashes onto the hologram behind the auctioneer who whistles in appreciation.

"Number 8 at a whopping one hundred and sixty five million. I repeat..."

My client is grinning, leaning back in his chair.

"Number 25 has raised it to one hundred and seventy million. Oh my. I repeat, Number 25 at one hundred and seventy million!" The auctioneer chants in amazement.

The room is silent; my client is slack-jawed, staring at the hologram in absolute astonishment, astounded by the sheer amount. No one makes any more bids.

"Oh, wow. I guess the auction is over. I'm Murray: Sarah Murray. It's been a pleasure..." she says, as she extends her hand.

"McCoy, Charlie McCoy, and the pleasures all mine, Ms. Murray," I say as I shake her hand.

"Number 25 has successfully purchased this lot at the remarkable price of one hundred and seventy million dollars. Give a round of applause..." the auctioneer shouts.

"Hopefully, you'll feel the sun a lot more from now on," I say.

She tilts her head in confusion.

"... for Charlie McCoy! Congratulations!"

ALEX KERR

Sky Full of Stars

At first people thought it was beautiful, all these new stars appearing every night. I did. I especially liked that in cities you could see the stars for the first time. Some nights when I would leave the office late, I could see them on my way through downtown Chicago, shining down between the tall dark shadows of buildings.

However, after a couple of months, people started to realise there were more and more stars each night. The night sky above the small apartment we lived in seemed to blaze like white fire. Josh, when I accidentally woke him up one night at 12:15 a.m. having just arrived home, said, "It seems like it's hot at night, doesn't it?" After that, it didn't seem just pretty, anymore.

You could see stars during the day. People said we were falling towards the galactic centre. Scientists claimed it was nothing, that there'd been a period of intense star formation 13 billion years ago, and we were only now seeing the result, but they didn't seem to believe it. The more religious people prayed like there was no tomorrow. Others postponed having kids.

It'll probably be any day now, we tell each other. We sit on the porch wearing sunscreen to ward off star burn, as people are calling it, saying, "We'll probably realise why it's happening, pretty soon."

Eventually I say I have to get up early to drive to the office, so we go to bed, drawing the curtains over the wall of light that never goes away.

Worth This

For the first time in my life, I wonder if I made the right choice. Was it worth this? Was power worth the pain? Was the journey worth the loss?

The beautiful, sorrowful night suffocates me.

Still, I can see the body of Air kneeling over Earth and I tighten my grip on Earth's pendant in my hand, trying to wake up.

Only I know this is real.

And I will never forget it.

The scenes from earlier today replay in my head…

*

The sun was directly above us, our shadows very small. The four of us were standing together, creating a little circle. Earth, who was on my right, was fidgeting nervously. She kept playing with her necklace. The pendant was catching the sunrays; the emerald stone was shining. I fingered my own pendant, round and silver, just like Earth's but with a sapphire stone instead. Fire's stone was an orange topaz, and Air's was a diamond. Our lifelines, we called them. Without them, our powers would be lost. They were the source of our inhuman strength.

Earth reached out and clasped Air's hand for comfort. I searched for Fire's hand.

I smiled to myself, thinking of the phrase, 'opposites attract.' That seemed to be true for us. Earth and Air. Fire and me.

I glanced down at my feet, trying to focus. I went through what we'd prepared.

It was all for today.

A low rumble made me lift my head, and glance around.

We stood together, one last time, saying one last goodbye.

Our enemy, Darkness approached, leading his army. Darkness was the adversary of light, therefore the adversary of us.

A low growl came from Fire. We lined up, side by side, ready. We'd prepared for this our whole lives.

Fire started to glow, his hands forming flames.

Earth spread her arms; her hands faced the ground, which started trembling.

Air was slowly rising, his feet above the ground as the sky darkened and growled.

I looked behind me at the lake that we purposefully stood in front of. It started churning violently, forming a deadly wave. My hands were cooling, ready to shoot out water.

Darkness stared at us from under his black hood.

I raised my hands, and forced my wave above and over us. The water knocked over the oncoming army. The lightning started to electrocute them. Air was flying over the soldiers, aiming bolts at them. Earth started to make the ground move, and cracks opened. A few soldiers fell into the pit. Fire was shooting flames at the soldiers who had escaped the water and lightning. His body was glowing like embers. I could feel the air around him sizzling.

Not wanting to interfere with Fire's flames by neutralising our powers, I took off in a different direction, with more soldiers coming towards me. I sped up and jumped, jumped higher than possible, landing on top of a soldier, pushing him down. The water in my control literally dissolved him. His staff was left on the ground. I lifted it up, blocking a few soldiers. I pushed another away before using only a little of my strength to throw one into the sky. Air flew past and caught him, throwing him towards the ground. The same soldier burst into flames before being enveloped by the ground.

I grinned to myself – we *were* powerful.

Things seemed to happen in slow motion, everything was too easy. Yet it all happened so fast. I almost began to enjoy myself.

It was raining, thanks to Air. I used the raindrops to form a water funnel, and pushed it through a group of soldiers. Seeing some more advancing, I turned and dived into the lake. I felt myself being charged by the water. Relaxing, I breathed deeply underwater as soldiers started jumping in. I formed a protective water bubble around me and waited…

Air's lightning bolt sizzled everything else in the water.

I laughed.

At one point, I'd run out of soldiers to destroy, so I started to walk towards Earth to help her.

That was when it happened.

Earth was forming roots that were trapping and stabbing soldiers. One threw his spear at her, but luckily, Air's quick reflexes blew it off course. Earth moved sideways to let it fly by, but the staff caught her necklace that was flapping in the wind.

I watched helplessly as her pendant, her lifeline, blew off and disappeared into the soil.

At once, Earth's powers vanished. The roots she had formed broke away as the ground became still. No more cracks appeared. Earth was powerless.

My heart thumped as I watched Earth's eyes widen. Air flew towards her. She turned to her right, and started sprinting, heading for Air. He was flying as fast as he could, speeding towards the ground, arms outstretched. Earth was visibly weakening as her stride slowed. She reached her hand up to let Air sweep her off the surface, away from danger.

He didn't reach her in time.

With only two metres between them, something slim sailed towards Earth.

A soldier's spear flew through her heart.

Earth's momentum let her fall forward. Air, still flying fast, caught Earth as her limp body collapsed towards him. He stumbled across the ground, Earth cradled in his arms.

"NO!"

The fury and anger in Air's voice was a sound I'd never heard before. His rage exploded. Lightning blasted. Thunder screamed. Gusts of wind propelled.

I was blown backwards, helpless as Air's powers were at the maximum.

The remaining soldiers had all disappeared before I could even see through the storm. Darkness had too. But I didn't care. I wiped my tears and ran towards Earth's body, as did Fire. Air lowered her gently to the ground. His strength evaporated as did his storm. The weather cleared and the beautiful sunset blinded me for a moment.

Air gently pulled out the spear, and placed it aside. Earth was still breathing, but barely. Her copper hair was starting to wither like grass. Her emerald eyes were fading, the brightness weakening like dying flowers. The blood on her chest was spreading like water on dirt. Air took her hand. His grey eyes were already wet.

When I got there, I sat next to Fire, and held Earth's other hand. I pushed water out of my palm, hoping to rejuvenate Earth. Earth needed water to grow. Maybe water would heal. All that happened was that Earth's breathing slowed.

"No!" I cried.

Fire took my shaking body, and held me close as I screamed in agony. Air's tears were falling onto Earth's hair. He leant down and kissed her forehead.

Earth's chest stopped rising.

*

"Goodbye Earth," I whisper and I place her pendant, which I found, in her cold palm.

Fire stands next to me. "Goodbye, the Earth we knew."

We walk away, hand in hand, to let Air say goodbye.

Was it worth this? I do not know.

RUSSELL BOEY

As the Scriptures Said

The world ended in fire, just as the scriptures of the Old Faith had said it would.

I had been told myths before, of a wonderful and green place, where there had been strange things called trees that had sprouted strange things called leaves. It's unbelievable, I think.

The Earth we knew, the Earth that we had known since we had been born, was something that could just as easily have gone by another name from the Old Faith; one which had been described as a place of eternal suffering where the Dragon and all of his spawn would be sent away to.

Well, the Dragon had never come, and here we all were still, thinking that the world could damn well end without his help.

In our small group of wanderers, we had only ever had two who remembered anything of the Old Earth. We had access to exactly one weapon, one of those strange sharp sticks, which seemed to have some veins running along its edge. I'd never mastered it. The children, like me, had never been told exactly what had happened that had caused weapons to be in such high demand – something to do with explosions, a war that had started and ended at about the same time, and then this. This place that belonged more to monsters than men.

One of the elders said that it was something to do with a change in some sort of code, caused by the war, which meant nothing to me, since I had never used code in my life.

As far as I was concerned, there were two-headed furred beasts, and massive scaled things walking around, and that was it.

For that reason we wandered, as I have always wanted, scarcely daring even to light a fire for fear of attracting the beasts. If that happened, there was only one person who could defend us from them.

On this night, there was a fire. It had seemed safe enough at the time, and all the children were glad of it. I was nearing that age at which I began to take some interest in speaking with the adults, though I was still accepted by the children. Tonight I sat with the adults. One of the elders was rambling on about the Old World again.

"Back then," said she, in such a wistful voice that I began to listen more closely, "there weren't abominations like these things; no behemoths, or such. There were dogs and lizards, small and wonderful creatures..."

"You don't need to taunt us with tales of such a paradise," said a glum, somewhat sardonic voice from the circle of adults.

The voice was like stone grating, and that was what the man heralded, because he was the Azrael, named after some sort of creature from the Old Faith as well. He was the only one with access to the weapon, and he was the only one who could use it well. Most people would have been happy to do away with his cynical comments and the unending cloud of grimness that surrounded him; a cloud which I thought seemed all too happy to break away in clumps and circle other people around the Azrael.

There were two reasons that he hadn't been thrown out: the first was that he was the only source of defence that we had against any of the beasts, and the second was that everyone had decided that it would end badly if they tried to forcefully evict him.

When the Azrael said something, everyone would try their best not to contradict him. The adults fell to talking of other things, which failed to hold my attention.

That night was the most important night of my life, but in truth my own recollection of it is somewhat hazy. I know that I stayed up for far longer than I should have, and by the time everything interesting happened I was far too tired to know exactly what was going on. At some point through the night, there was a loud roaring, and the Azrael had said something about how foolish we were to have lit a fire.

The roaring was still ringing in my ears, and I heard absolutely nothing that happened next. I saw that the fire was put out, and people started running. I myself got somewhat lost, and flailed wildly around in the darkness for a time. I imagined that this was probably what it was like to be drunk – something that few people ever experienced now.

A few moments later, I could see a bright glow as the weapon kicked into power. It shone with a green, almost fluorescent sheen, illuminating the Azrael, who held the blade poised to strike.

And something else.

I had never seen a behemoth before that night, and I still wish that I hadn't. But I think that I'll be seeing a lot more in my life. The creature's long, sinuous body and massive reptilian head reminded me of the herald of the end of the world, the Dragon that the Old Faith had foretold. It was not the most pleasant thought when the creature was bearing down on you.

I ended up scrabbling up a hill before tripping, and rolling back to about the same place where I had started. The Azrael was certainly not in the same place. He had been flung backwards without his blade, which, I realised, was glowing right beside me. I could see the form of the behemoth as it slowly paced towards him, mouth wide open. I felt like one of the feet was about to land on me. So I grabbed for the glowing blade. Then a lot of things happened at once.

I saw a beam of green light. Then I heard a roar, and the Azrael running at me, grabbing me. Finally I saw the creature keel over.

I had just killed a behemoth. Accidentally, but it was me.

There is some sort of tradition with us: anyone who does the job of the Azrael is the Azrael.

So here I am now – the next Angel of Death.

The Earth We Knew

It is metal, the Earth we know
And hardness and darkness and slow.
Painful
Death
Life fades into skeletons.
We are all skeletons,
Such silent submissive skeletons.
They say,
"Keep quiet."
       "Keep still."
           "Shut up."
"Back down."
     "It's loaded."
Click

Now there's a girl
A dull brown piece of driftwood
Torn apart by the storm
Of metal and blood and silence.
She lives in this storm, a shattered orb,
A gunshot wounded world.
And in this orb
She dreams.
And for this dream she could cry a river
For the Earth we know,
For the Earth we knew,
For the Earth we cannot call back.

One with the Earth

We belong to the Earth,
And the Earth is ours,
Every blade of grass,
The trees, the flowers,
The lakes and rivers,
The sticks and stones,
It's our blood and muscle,
Our skin and bones.

So why, may I ask,
Do we cut down trees?
Would you do the same to your loved one?
Bring them to their knees?
Would you beat them to nothing?
Burn them down?
Make them bleed?
Make them frown?

This here is the present,
It's all we know.
But I'll tell you of a time,
When plants used to grow.
Oh, how they'd flourish,
We thought it all would last.
This, my friends,
This was the past.

A time and place,
Where the Earth was its own,
No buildings or roads,
Nothing man-made, only grown.
The beauty was natural,
The life was pure.

There was no need for mechanics.
Were they really the cure?

So sit up and listen,
Have a look around.
Can you hear the wind blowing?
Or has even that been bound?
Only now we realize,
What we have done,
What we cost the Earth,
Because we thought it was fun.

We belong to the Earth,
And the Earth is ours,
Every blade of grass,
The trees, the flowers.
We can fix our mistakes,
Once again we'll be free.
I am the Earth,
The Earth is me.

The Cure

United Nation, Auckland, 2040

The solution was miniscule, about five hundred milligrams. It was small, but important. It would be a platform to raise the Earth from its current slump. It would bring the kings to their knees, and bring the power back to the people. Professor Albert Quill had to get it out of the laboratory.

He strolled quickly out of the lab, flashing his ID to the guard who gave him a casual nod of the head. His footsteps clacked lightly on the linoleum floor of the lobby, as he made his way to the street. A white officer was stationed at the street corner. Professor Quill ducked behind one of the new hydrogen powered taxis. The officer glanced in his direction, and then shifted his gaze to the traffic. There were cars powered by oxygen, hydrogen, helium, and even nitrogen.

Professor Quill saw one of the sickos; the name was cruel, but not inaccurate. This man was in stage three; his skin tone was that of butter. It would be green by the end of the week. The rainbow disease worked in seven stages. The first stage was the red skin which would advance to orange skin, then yellow skin, etc. This disease affected thirty percent of the United Nation, and Albert Quill had the cure in his coat pocket.

The pill was wrapped in a cheap paper towel from the bathroom. The pill was pure black, the darkest kind Quill had ever seen.

He worried about the officers seeing him. He had had previous trouble for acts of defiance against the Nation. The first, many years before, was for donating fifty cents to a sicko. He had committed various other crimes including harbouring sickos for research, and even protecting a woman from a particularly aggressive officer.

Rounding a corner, he passed a sign read: IT IS ILLEGAL TO AID SICKOS IN ANY WAY. Next to it, another sign displayed the top ten most wanted fugitives. He was number five.

I've been improving, he thought to himself.

He scanned the list for the rest of the pricks who were lucky enough to land themselves on this list.

Ryder Robertson was still number one; no surprise.

Ryder was a pro-sicko activist whose mother had died from the disease.

On the 6th February 2034, he had committed the biggest single act of terrorism ever witnessed in the Nation. He and three members had climbed the sky tower. At three o'clock the asteroids began. They fired rocket launcher shots from the observation deck for twenty minutes before they used wing suits to leave the scene.

Ryder was hiding somewhere the Nation found it hard to send officers – the bush. Regular YouTube videos indicated the so called 'soldier for sickos' was coming back with a vengeance.

Quill was no mercenary, and he certainly wasn't a 'soldier for the sickos.' He had just wanted the accolades. Hell. He had wanted to feel important. Key word 'had.' The reason the government would not like his pill was they already had a cure. Their cure had been around for a while, and was much cheaper than Quill's. A bullet to the head.

The government used the fear produced from the illness; they used it like Ryder had used those asteroids. Their weapons were much more subtle, but way more destructive. A candidate who had promised tough action on the sickos would be twenty-four times more likely to win an election than a candidate who was lax on the invalids. A prime example was the mayor of Auckland, Tim

Larsson, whose major boozing and womanising had been ignored because of his promises to segregate schools.

Quill got into a hydrogen-powered taxi with an image of Larsson on the side. The driver was a white man with a thick moustache and a balding scalp.

"Hey bud where ya going?" the driver asked, a cigarette hanging from the corner of his mouth.

"Do you know Aroha?" Doubt coloured Quill's voice.

"Yeah, sure bud. My mum lives out there. It's gonna be a bit," the driver warned.

"That's fine, mate," Quill assured. The driver pulled into the traffic, not noticing as the car behind did the same.

*

Officer Steve Sims had risen quickly through the ranks of the Nation's police force. He was considered somewhat of a hotshot, and his colleagues didn't like him for it. But that didn't matter now. Watching the car in front, Sims knew he was about to make the biggest arrest of his life. The young hotshot was gonna show those pricks above, in their captain's uniforms.

He followed the taxi, being careful not to alert the occupants.

*

Up ahead the driver glanced at his passenger in the mirror.

"Hey you're that bloke the government wants," he said in alarm.

Quill pulled his side-arms out of his holsters. He pressed one of the ruby-infused pistols to the driver's skull.

"Ok, now listen," Quill started.

"Holy shit," the driver exclaimed.

"No buddy, that's not what you're gonna do. You're going to drop me off at the gas station, and then you're gonna drive away," Quill explained slowly as if talking to a child.

The driver nodded.

Following at a distance, Sims decided to call for back-up. By the time Quill got out of the taxi, four patrol cars were behind Sims. Sims pulled out his hydraulic-pistol.

The gas station had been in Quill's family for three generations. Quill was unlucky; in an era of gas-powered cars, he was like a CD when IPods came out. IPods were outdated now; Apple had just announced a chip that, once inserted into someone's brain, provided free music forever.

The police opened fire as soon as he got out of his vehicle. He returned the shots. One of his bullets struck Sims in the shoulder, making him sprawl on his back.

Quill dived through the doors, and ran upstairs to the girl in the bedroom. The girl on the bed was skeletal. She was in the blue stage. Her skin reminded him of barren seawater.

"Dad," she panted.

"Hi, darling, you need to listen to me."

"Ok," she whispered.

"Take this pill, and don't question me, alright?"

She took the pill from him, and managed to swallow it, despite her pain.

"Now darling, you will have to raise yourself. I can't be your protector any more. This is not the Earth I knew. It is dangerous. Just remember, I will always love you, and that you know how to help the sickos."

He dropped the small scrap of paper at her side, and turned to head back down the stairs.

TOBEY MORRISON

The Immunisation

Like everyone else, I was immunised when I was eight. On my eighth birthday, I was taken into a cold, sterile room that held nothing but a chair, a robotic doctor, and a window allowing me to stare at the aphotic, cloud-packed sky.

"Sit. Hold out your arm. The needle will be inserted for two hours; long enough that the medical chip will find its way into your system, but not too long that it cuts through your bones," Dr Robot stated without blinking.

"O-okay; it doesn't hurt, right?" My voice betrayed my dread.

"No," she said.

Did she even have a personality, a heart, anything...? When the needle punctured the skin I realised she was a liar as much as she was a bore. The thin silver bullet hit me fast and forceful. I sat immobile in the chair while Mrs Robot droned on about the dangers of Colta disease. She said everything she could to scare me. My brain was hacked open, and all happy thoughts were exchanged for nauseating details of what would happen if we didn't have the immunisation.

"If there were to be a Colta outbreak," she told me, "it would affect everybody differently."

She familiarized me with the one Colta case in all of history, a twelve year old girl who developed it in her bones. Over three days it ate her cartilage, leaving her a gelatinous mess. Mrs Robot's mouth kept moving, but I wasn't listening. All I saw was the girl, powerless and dying. By the time the needle was extracted I was walking paranoia; I knew I had been immunised and should feel safe. But that's just who I am, obsessive and anxious.

Eight years later, and fear of Colta disease had been replaced with the fear of being tracked and watched. Starting school at nine, I fell instantly in love with Computer Science. When I fixed somebody's computer they labelled me a hero; the sensation I had was so powerful I realised that I craved being the centre of attention. I taught myself to hack, and never looked back. I had found my passion, my escape; I could happily hack computers every second of every day.

It was also the death of me, literally. I had developed a new fear, which I never told anyone about. They would call it lunacy, or even worse, rebellion.

My anxiety was fuelled by a multitude of blocked sites on the World Government Web. I found one called Tracked, which explained that the immunisation was really a bug the government used to track us. The worst part was that Colta disease was made up to scare us and keep us from rebelling. People from all over submitted their own "conspiracy evidence." The more I read, the more I believed. I even experienced conspiracy myself.

I'd gotten home from school and headed for the phone.

"Call Ellie Bluelei," I said.

She'd just been on a trip to the moon, and I couldn't wait to hear how it went.

"Hel-lo, Ellie here," Ellie's annoying voice greeted me.

"How was it?" My voice dripped anticipation.

"It was A-M-A-Z-I-N-G," she shrieked. "The rocket was great. They told me to close my eyes because of the altitude or something, but guess what? I DIDN'T!" She giggled like a two year old.

I laughed. "That's what I call some serious rebellion."

At that moment, the line shut off, and my arm vibrated like a phone. It was hardly the strongest evidence, but to me it made all the difference. I'd sat there for years, on my cushioned swivel chair, reading about this conspiracy theory, believing it, knowing it was true, and not doing anything. Now I'd had my epiphany. I had to do something.

Waking at midnight, I pulled on my black jeans, long-sleeved t-shirt, and balaclava, and sneaked out. I didn't care about the trouble I would be in; I knew I would be thanked – I would be a hero to all. Someday the government would activate the trackers to the next level, turning all immunised humans into mindless clones. I'd read it in every website. It was going to happen. It was only a matter of time.

I jumped onto my hoverboard, and flew off towards Government Central. Parking a few metres from the immense building, I slipped through the shadows, and hoisted myself onto a ledge. Using my grip-shoes to crawl to the top, I jumped through a window and into the computer room. It all seemed ridiculously easy. I had prepared for worse, but I wasn't complaining.

"You'll save everyone," I kept telling myself. "You'll be a hero."

There were no guards in the room, nor any cameras or lasers. Where was the security? I sat at a terminal and typed furiously. I was desperate; I could become the centre of attention of the world.

After a minute of frenzied typing a large banner slid across the screen. "WOULD YOU LIKE TO DE-ACTIVATE THE CODE FOR THE COLTA VACCINATION CHIP?"

With feverish fingers I typed, "YES."

"ARE YOU SURE YOU WOULD LIKE TO DE-ACTIVATE THE CODE FOR THE COLTA VACCINATION CHIP?"

"You mean the tracker chip," I said aloud

It all ended. Everything.

I was knocked from my chair, but not by a guard. A black stain spread across my body. I was dying; dying from Colta disease. My breaths were slow yet desperate, my mind racing. My very existence flashed before my eyes; the immunisation was real. Colta disease – was real.

Nobiliteranceol disease was real also. People diagnosed with it became obsessed with heroism, and believed in anything that could help them find glorification. If I had lived long enough I would have known that I had Nobiliteranceol. I would have known that I had killed everyone. I had de-activated the very chip that kept them alive. I would have known that websites like Tracked were full of fake stories from disgusting people like me, people that craved and required attention.

Colta disease was like a gust of wind that blew constantly through our air. As soon as I de-activated the chip its tendrils of sickness engulfed every person I intended to free, killing them as easily as blowing on a speck of dust.

I will never know why my arm vibrated that time when I called Ellie and said "Rebellion." Maybe I'd imagined it, or maybe the government wanted to keep an eye on people like me, for the safety of the world.

That hadn't worked.

I'd never know why there hadn't been any guards that night. Whatever the case I clung to the thought that what I had done wasn't so abominable as I drifted into a bed of flames.

Someday, when the ashes of our once fruitful lives have well and truly settled, a single flower will begin to grow, and with that flower, will come the beginning of a whole new world. The Earth we knew will become an ant in the galaxy.

Echolalia

The early morning sun burned her eyes.

Thisbe stood in front of the trunk of the car as she attempted to type out a last text message. Her parents yelled for her to hurry from the front seats. The bustling of traffic was beginning in the distance. Thisbe threw her phone into her open bag on the ground, zipped it up, and heaved up on the straps.

There was a horrible, grating sound of metal against metal.

Thisbe stumbled back, pulling the bag away from the car.

"Oops."

*

"Dad, you're going the wrong way!"

Thisbe was thrown hard against the door as Frank swerved to fix his mistake.

"Give your sister the map," he said, gripping the wheel tightly.

The trees blurred past. The sun cast its last muted rays along the ridges of the far away hills.

"But…"

"Frank," her mother said over Nadia. "Nadia has her hands full with the fixing the GPS that *you* broke."

Frank glanced at Meredith, who had placed her delicate fingers on the bridge of her nose.

"Besides," Meredith went on smoothly, "we're on the right path now."

A horrifying wheeze echoed from Nadia. Concerned, Thisbe looked over to her sister just as Nadia jerked her head up from the GPS.

"*Pothole!*" Nadia screamed wide-eyed. It was the first word she had spoken all day.

Thisbe cringed. Nadia's voice was like broken glass, piercing the quiet hum of their car.

Frantically, Frank wrenched on the wheel, avoiding the giant ditch in the road.

He hadn't even cleared a few metres down the side route when another car shot out from the intersection. Frank slammed down on the brakes, but not before the other car skimmed their bumper, scaring a scream out of Meredith.

The other car continued without pause. Frank rolled down the window like his life depended on it.

"Learn to drive!" he roared into the night.

The car was already long gone.

Frank jerked the car back onto the road.

Nadia retreated back into her little nook.

Night had fallen. Only the road ahead was visible; a smooth black blanket shrouded everything the headlights couldn't touch.

"Nadia?" Thisbe tried.

No answer.

Thisbe turned her head away, gazing out the window again.

They rolled to a stop under the red of a dilapidated traffic light.

There was only the clicking and beeping of Nadia's GPS as they waited.

"That's weird," Frank said after a while.

"That the light isn't changing?" Meredith said.

"No," he said, fiddling with the dashboard. "The clock has stopped. The digital display is supposed to run on the battery."

"Well, what did I tell you about buying second-hand?" Meredith muttered under her breath. Louder, she said, "Just go. There aren't any cars coming, and there's a queue building up behind us."

Thisbe startled. She swivelled around to see dozens of headlights beaming back at her through the rear window.

"At this hour?"

"Let's go, Frank!" Meredith snapped.

Frank pushed down on the pedal, and ran the red light.

Thisbe leant down to examine the map again. Squinting, she held the map closer, unsure if she was imagining the lines and colours almost blurring together, or if it were a trick of the light. She rubbed her eyes, holding back a yawn.

Frank pressed down on the gas slowly. He rolled up his window, abandoning any attempts to stick his head out to distinguish some bearings outside.

"Thisbe, where are we going?"

"Um…" Thisbe forced herself to focus, but for the strangest moment, she couldn't keep her gaze on the map. "Straight ahead."

"Are you sure?" Her father glanced back for a moment. "Because…"

In a flash, the interior of car illuminated in white light.

"Frank, watch out!" Meredith screamed.

Frank didn't react fast enough, but thankfully, the other car did. Thisbe's hand flew to her heart as the other car screeched in its haste to stop.

Faintly, an angry male voice yelled something out at them. Thisbe could have sworn it had said *Learn to drive!*

"This is why you keep your eyes on the road!" Meredith chided.

Frank made a noise deep in his throat. "Nothing happened, did it? I know what I'm doing."

Thisbe blinked. Once. Twice. Had she heard correctly?

"Thisbe, directions," Frank snapped, bringing her back.

Thisbe glanced down.

She thought the main road kept going straight, though if she was honest, she had already lost track of where they were. She wished Nadia would hurry up with the GPS.

She held the map up to the bare-bone moonlight that clutched at the horizon.

"Take the next left that comes up."

They drove for what felt like eons, bumping along gravel, and then back onto smooth ground. Nadia had begun humming a cheery tune, taking the batteries from the GPS and shaking the device.

Thisbe winced.

"Are you nearly done?" she asked her sister gently.

Nadia looked at her. Blinked. Shrugged.

Thisbe crossed her arms, and leaned against her seat. They slowed down as a queue appeared before them.

"Where are all these cars coming from?" Frank said, tapping his thumb against the wheel.

"There must be another light ahead," Meredith said.

Seconds ticked by, but the queue did not move. The vehicles stretching ahead of them were uniform mounds of dark shadows under the weak shine of the waxing moon now high in the night.

Thisbe frowned, undoing her seatbelt.

"Dad," she said, leaning into the front. "Turn your headlights to full beam."

Frank furrowed his eyebrows. "May I ask why?"

Thisbe reached over, and did it herself.

The car in front had the exact same scratch at the base, sitting just to the right of the number plate.

DED129

They also had the exact same number plate.

Slowly Thisbe dipped the headlights, and sat back in her seat. If she peered closely, she could see movement in the car in front; a silhouette in the backseat reaching over to their companion.

She couldn't quite tell if it was a hug, or attempted strangulation.

Thisbe's hands were shaking as she attempted to open her door. It did not budge, not even when she thumped her foot against the bottom.

"What the hell is this?" Frank demanded.

The only answer was Nadia starting a staccato rhythm against the dark screen of the GPS with her fingers.

She was mumbling something over and over again. Thisbe was so surprised at this conscious stream of sound that she leaned closer to hear what her sister was trying to say.

"Nothing else remains on the Earth we knew."

Thisbe scrambled away, gasping for air, smashing her fists against the window. Ten, twenty attempts, and they just kept bouncing back like it was rubber rather than glass.

Another car rumbled into the space behind them, stopping. Its headlights lit through their rear window as the beam turned up to full, and then dipped again.

Thisbe screamed.

DANA SMAGGE

Toxic Roots

There was no way to tell what was to happen next. No one expected it from her. She seemed so calm, so together. She always got to class on time, made good marks, she was an average teenager. There was no way to tell that she was slowly suffocating.

It has been three days since the incident. We were best friends since primary, yet I'm only now realizing that I didn't know her at all. I thought I did. It's weird how you can go ages without noticing something until it's put right in front of you. I thought things were fine; everyone did. But now that I look back, I notice the small comments, the far away looks, all the little things that were tiny glimpses of what she was really feeling. I think all the time about how I could have changed what happened. If only once I had questioned her on her strange comments.

Just last Tuesday we were sitting in maths, and she was off on one of her rants.

I remember her saying "The Earth isn't going to last much longer you know. There's these wacky plants, Phragmites, that have these roots that are so toxic they kill all the surrounding plants."

She was interested in all kinds of strange nature facts, especially ones that were bad for the Earth. She had all sorts of rocks and plants in her room, but the thing that gets me now is what she said next, the thing that will haunt me for the rest of my life.

"You know the Earth and me, we aren't that different really."

The school sent me to the guidance counsellor today. I was asked all kinds of questions about what happened. It still seems like fiction to me. It feels as if she's just gone on another family holiday, and she will be back any day now. Day after day I can imagine her walking through the classroom door like usual. But the days continue to go by, and she still doesn't come back. She can't come back. Even if she could, I get the feeling she wouldn't want to. She was always talking about those Phragmites that could kill Earth. Maybe she had some too.

I walk home alone. A simple task that feels empty without her. Her on the grass, me on the footpath, we would just walk and talk. She would tell me about her latest plant, and I would talk about what happened in science. Everything seemed so normal. I guess that's what makes it so bad, you don't really notice until it's too late. The Phragmites dig in their roots and just grow and grow, poisoning everything in their path with their toxins.

I think back to what she said that day; "The Earth and me aren't that different."

She was like the Earth in a way. The Earth we knew was dying, and we were too busy with ourselves to notice she was overrun with Phragmites.

NADIA SNEGIREV

Dear Earth

The Earth we knew,
We mourn for you.

I miss your emotional turmoil,
Your crashing waves
And your bitter winds.

I miss your tranquillity,
Your silky water,
Your graceful flowers.

I miss our home you created
From our humble beginnings in your heart: the forest
To the skyscrapers, the new gods of the sky.

But we broke you.
We stripped you of your resources.
We chased away your children.
We filled your ocean with our artificial waste.

If you look out into the evening sky
And find the smallest star,
Around there is where we are.
I hope you'll whisper
I miss you, too.

Tomorrow

The Earth we knew,
The life that was,
No longer exists.

Cinnamon autumns glowed in yesterday's sepia,
A yesterday of friends and talks,
Melted ice-cream and long walks
In the park
Where evenings of chatter
Stretched long into the indigo nights.
The life we knew;
Of politicians, debates,
And beeswax,
Held the excitement, the promise
Of tomorrow.

The Earth we knew no longer exists
Because tomorrow came,
But in clouds of dust.
And we watched as the lazy summers
passed
       into
         darkness.
Tomorrow brought black twisted smoke
In tortured screams.
Gravel crunching,
Quick footsteps,
A knife in the back,
Dark silhouettes in the streets;
Roads of graffiti

And rubber.
Tomorrow brought tanks and guns,
Faces of ash
And pale, wide eyes.
Only hoping for a different tomorrow
For the Earth we knew.

The life that was,
No longer exists.
We escaped into those once indigo skies.
Set adrift from a planet of flame.
Burnt and blackened, it slowly faded
    into
            the distance.
Our children knew only of void,
Of wires and quiet.
Yet we longed for that
Peppermint grass,
The long walks in the park
But we laughed at the madman,
With his wife left behind.
As he attempted to create
The life that was.

Still he built in his lab
A world of ocean and green,
With indigo skies and sepia autumns.
A world so big with promise
Yet so small in space.
It was the Earth.

         Wee.
            New.

AMY HUANG

Bedtime Stories

"The Earth we knew..."
four words
start my bedtime story.

Imagination projected on metal bunk panels:
forests with tendrils of organic imperfections,
like veins on the storyteller's wrinkled hands.

The oxygen meter bar
shrinks steadily
to a small box.

Rectangle like two frames on my bunker wall:
the expanse of a fifteen by twenty centimetre safari,
Grandpa's animated smile, boxed and frozen.

The faded images
hide away
Grandpa's bedtime stories.

Imagination blocking noises of crickets and wind:
twigs made into rocket ships and space stations,
like the metal box where the little boy was trapped.

Route 666

It was the third time this week someone had taken Frankie's lunch money. And he wasn't even at school yet. He'd fought back the first few times, but his Mum's crestfallen face when she saw Frank's black eye sobered him up to reality. Frankie was small, and small people got pummelled. It didn't matter though; Pete always had a ton of whatever slightly expired concoction his Aunt had whipped up that week.

Frank looked up from his sulking to loud shouting in the seats in front him. It was 7:30 in the morning, but Alex still seemed to have the energy to piss people off.

"Alexander Williams, sit your loud mouth *down* before I call the exterminators!" barked the driver, turning away from the wheel angrily, one arm slung over the back of her chair.

Alex flicked her off before moodily sliding in beside Frank. Frank slouched back in his threadbare grey seat, and stared out the window. Even after all these years, he still kept up the loose hope that something interesting might pop up in the empty desert landscape.

Whoever thought it was a good idea to build a school in the outer districts clearly didn't have to endure the hour bus ride to get there.

Wind whipped up the sandy dirt outside as the bus rumbled along the road at a painfully slow speed. Government funding had been cut by 60% and they'd had to revert to the Toyota models last used when California counted as a state. But at least they had transport and a radio. The desert could be deadly without a radio.

The bus had been going so slowly he hadn't even realized it had stopped. The driver swore loudly before getting up and clambering out of the booth.

"Listen up, brats. The motor's given out; radio transmission's down, so I'm gonna try get help from Anthrax Station."

That was 3 miles away; Frankie gave a quiet fist pump at the hope of missing at least a half day of school.

Pulling up the bandanna she had wrapped around her thick reddened neck, the driver exited the bus in heavy thumping footsteps. Once she was fully lost in the haze of blowing sand, the junior kids ran over to the window, and pressed their hands and noses against the glass anxiously.

"Frankie man, come sit," Pete yelled back from the passenger seat.

Frank clambered over Alex, who was trying to scoop up something powdery-looking from the floor, and almost tripping over Victoria who was busy carving some kind of insignia into the seat. When he finally made it to the front, Pete was looking at some tatty paperback and fiddling with the ignition slot.

"She forgot to take the radio," he commented with a sniff.

Frank froze. "SHE FORGOT TO TAKE THE RADIO," he screamed at the kids over the seat.

Even if transmission was down, going into the desert without a radio could be fatal. This was bad. This was so bad.

"What do you mean she didn't take the radio," Alex yelled back from the aisle, where he was propped on his elbows.

"I mean, that the radio," Frank said slowly, holding up the offending device, "was left under Pete's skinny butt."

"It'll be fine," Veronica said uncertainly, turning to the juniors. "She'll get a tracking signal back at Anthrax."

The bus erupted into arguments. Frank wrung his hands nervously; they'd be found, just as long as the tracker was still working. But in this kind of weather it was unlikely.

The sandstorms had never stopped long enough for roads to be built outside of the inner city, but the packed sand was firm enough to drive on anyway. This did mean, however, that the only way to find people out here was a tiny, sand-clogged location transmission device that was glued to the windscreen. The trackers had a terrible history, and if it wasn't working, and the radio didn't come live again soon, they were stuffed.

Yelling from the back of the bus brought Frank back to reality. "What is it now?" He glared back at them moodily.

"It's a sandstorm!" Veronica screeched, pointing a trembling finger towards the window.

A massive wave of white sand rolled towards them; endless, bright and dry.

"Everyone to the left. Grab something, and don't let go," Alex bellowed, herding the juniors to the side.

"Frank!" Pete knocked him out of the trance, grabbing his arm and rolling them onto the floor, just as the bus began to tilt.

It was gentle at first, but after a few seconds, they were hit with a massive jolt. That's when it began to really fall over; the weight of 200 kilos of sand, and 30-odd kids was too much for the bus. They hit the ground hard. Someone was crying; someone was hurt. Frank was bleeding from being hit on the head by the gearstick.

"We have to call in. Maybe someone else has a radio," Pete muttered over the noise.

Behind them, Alex was walking on top of the windows-turned-floor, and picking people out of the entanglement of limbs. The sand-riddled wind blew hard and hot around them; rattling the walls and fogging up the skyward-facing windows. Alex gave them a pleading look, which said, "Is anyone on the radio line?"

Frank turned to Pete, who was lying on his side fiddling with the black box. "Anything?"

"Just static," he replied with a lump in his throat.

It was becoming hard to breathe without getting a mouthful of sand. The reality of the situation was sinking in, and it left everyone terrified and helpless. Nobody had trained them for this. This wasn't a world Frankie knew anything about. He wanted his old life back; the trees and the rain. He wanted before the plagues, and the sun heating up; before sandstorms and deserts. He wanted the world he knew; the world that was safe. The world that clearly wasn't here.

They both lay staring at the radio hopefully. But only white noise.

"Twiddle the knob thing," Alex shouted back distractedly.

"Thanks, Einstein," Pete yelled back haughtily.

"Just trying to help," Alex muttered.

Frank grabbed the radio from Pete, and held it up close to his ear. Something stuck out; it didn't quite seem like total white noise. He slowly turned the tuner to the side.

"Hello," he said. No reply. He tried again, turning the knob further. No reply. No reply. No reply. "Hello?"

The bus was almost totally dark now, packed in with sand, dirt, and low spirits. Sand was blowing in through gaps in the ceiling. Nobody spoke. The radio hummed. It gurgled and sparked.

"Hello?" Frank perked up, squinting at the box.

Then; a voice.

"Hello."

RANA CAWLEY

A Musical Theory

Part One: Outside

"Rodney! We can't get him to stop! He's declining!"

"Geez! Call me Rod. I'm going in."

White and blue. It's all I can see. I like blue. But not this blue. This is the doctor's blue. Thin skinny blue. Slicked onto their hands. Wrapped around their shiny tools. I like the blue sky. With white clouds. Not this.

"Graham! Get me my mask! I need to get in before he goes entirely!"

"This isn't going well, Rod. Why don't we just withdraw him?"

"I can't let this guy go. He feels like my only chance."

It doesn't register to me, the sound I hear. It just hurts. The sound is painful. I just want to go.

"Graham, you're my assistant. You specialize in this work. And you know you can't work anywhere else. This is a one-and-only job. We're on a trial, you know that, Graham!"

"Rod... You're putting our company at risk!"

"I know."

Some sound has gone. I feel like slipping. To a place with no white and blue.

"He's almost gone! I've got to get in."

I hear a small sound. The last bit of pain. Then I'm gone.

Part Two: In

I don't move. I don't *know* if I can move. It's dark and quiet. No painful noise. But no, I can't move. I'm scared now. Where am I? I want to yell, but my tongue feels like a thick wad of frozen sandpaper.

Suddenly, I hear sound, but it's not painful in the least. I hear footsteps, and I try to convince myself that I'm safe now, that someone is here, and now I can go back. But there I stop myself. Do I want to go back to that pain? I can't answer that now, because the footsteps are coming closer. Focus!

The footsteps stop. Something touches me. I can feel! It's warm, and I realize it's some*one*.

"Are you okay? Matthew?"

It's a man.

"Aah..." I say. I can't see the man; it's too dark.

"Good, you're talking. That's faster development than normal," he notes.

I can't do anything, so I just listen.

His tone is more serious now. "Matt, if you can hear me, you have to understand we're in a very dangerous situation now. Whatever you do, you're potentially putting both our lives at risk."

His words scare me, but his voice is calming, so I relax somewhat.

"Close your eyes, Matthew. Or is it Matt?"

"Matt," I mumble.

"Okay, Matt. Now think about a place you want to go. Anywhere you like."

I squeeze my eyes, then freeze. I'm scared I'll do something wrong. I think back to what he said mere seconds ago.

He feels me tense up. "Matt, don't panic."

I'm not, I want to say, but in reality, I am.

"Try again. Hold onto me tight, please."

I try to think of anything but this blackness. It's hard, but I see it. Blue. Blue sky and clouds. White clouds.

I feel the light before I open my eyes. I'm lying down on my back on a gritty surface; sand. Above I see the sky. I can move fine now, and so I roll onto my stomach.

"Matt! You did it!"

I flip back onto my back and find the man looking over me. He's fairly young; maybe about twice my age – twenty-six, perhaps. His long sandy-blond hair frames his striking blue eyes.

"Who are you and where am I?" This time I talk with ease, not even stuttering.

The man stands up, straightening, evidently proud.

"I'm Doctor Rod, and don't you know? We're both in your mind!"

I'm confused by this, and I must show it, because the doctor laughs.

"Never mind, of course you don't know. Stupid of me..." He turns away, muttering.

"Okay, I'll explain it straight," he says, turning back. "In our time, many doctors are finding that sometimes it's not drugs that help you get better. And obviously you want to diagnose the patients properly, with the Hippocratic Oath and all. But it's hard to do that; harder than you think."

The doctor plonks down on the yellow sand.

"I really shouldn't say anything more." He licks his lips.

"No, no! I need to hear this!" I'm trying hard to not sound desperate, but it doesn't work.

"I've got regulations, Matt, and I... "

"Please, doctor. Our lives might depend on it. You said so yourself."

"I..." He's having trouble eating his own words. "Oh, okay, but I'll regret it later."

I almost smile, but he looks so remorseful that I stop myself.

85

"It's an experiment. Theoretically, if this treatment works, it will change the Earth as we know it. It's where the trained doctor is released into the patient's mind. It's not fully tested, and you're not the first. We've had some others, but they've been slow, and they nearly killed me too. You see, *you* control everything here. You could conjure up a horse out of the sand and make it trample me. It's happened before."

The doctor pauses slightly.

"Matt, you are an experiment. You don't have any serious problems, though I doubt you were in tip-top shape as you entered. You should have been very disorientated."

No, I came out singing Yankee Doodle.

"What you do have, though, is quite a concerning phobia."

Oh no. This is what I wanted to get away from. Oh, no, no, no. I understand now.

"Matt, your phobia, what is it?"

I crumple into the sand.

"Sound. I'm scared of sound."

It's weak. I know it.

"These are my first conversations ever. The sound hurts me, and I hate it."

"Can you picture it?"

I shake my head. "No. I'm too scared I'll hurt you."

I look up, thinking the doctor will frown, but he grins.

"Matt, have you ever heard music?"

"No, doctor."

"Do you mind if I transfer an image from me to you?"

"Will it hurt?"

"I firmly believe not. Hold onto my arm, Matt."

I shut my eyes hard, and wait for the dark. Even through my eyelids, I see the light disappear. I keep my eyes closed, and only open them when I feel the light again.

"Matt, welcome to music."

I see people. They are dancing, wearing colourful costumes, soft, happy colours; colours I love. But what I hear is what changes something in me, not the colour. A beautiful sound. My legs move. My arms move. And I move for a long time to the sound I never loved.

Part Three: Clearer

The doctor's eyes fly open.

"Rod! The boy?"

The doctor grins. "Matt? He'll make it just fine. But you know I can't be around for this guy's awakening."

He gestures toward Matt. Graham nods, thumbs twiddling.

"Do me a small favour, Graham? Give this to him when he's fully conscious. Keep him comfortable until then, please."

The doctor hands Graham a small MP3 device with a headset.

"Cheers, Graham! Milk with your tea?"

Graham shudders. "No thanks."

The doctor laughs. "Looks like I already have another case on my hands."

Doctor Rodney walks out of the lab whistling.

RILEY JIM MCKEWEN

Round the World in Time

I thought it preposterous, and false beyond belief, but now that I have seen for myself, I can say to you it is most certainly correct. From voyaging for years I can say that the Earth we know is now the Earth we knew. What we have been taught, is false. If you are not already seated, I suggest you sit now as this is the most important thing that I will ever tell you; something you shall and will tell your children, and theirs. So listen closely because I will not say it again.

The Earth is *round!*

Not like the flat disc, or the wheel on your cart, but like the ball in the hands of a child. Yes! Everything we thought we knew is wrong. It opens up endless possibilities for discovery and exploration. I am sure you must know the danger of such a thought. I may be burnt, or worse…

Pardon?

Oh right, you wish for proof. Of course, you do!

As you know I have been absent for the last two years. What an expedition it was! I have sailed further than any before me, and yet, have never fallen over the edge of the Earth. Not once did I reach out and make contact with the horizon.

The discovery was made aboard our ship, the *Antikythera*, on the one-hundred-and-thirty-first day. It was then that my cartographer and navigator informed me that we had reached the position at which they had calculated the horizon to be when we set off. It was a joyous occasion! I immediately wished to sail further, but the men… the men were fearful. I made the decision to turn back, for the safety of both the body and mind of the crew.

Once back on shore I was abuzz, knowing that I could only tell someone I trust. That is why I travelled here so quickly to tell you, my dearest friend. You are the one I have chosen to entrust with this knowledge. I am glad you find what I have discovered so intriguing despite how it sounds coming from me, a respected and intelligent naval man. In truth, it scared me that I was the one to question the shape of our celestial body before any other man.

But I am! I am!

I know what you are saying, and yes, people have said this before I, but this is evidence as sturdy as the hull of the *Antikythera* herself! I intend to go beyond where I have left this to lie. I plan to sail from the seaport this coming May, and return without turning back, by sailing in a straight line around the Earth.

Translated from *'The Testimony of a Captain'* by Ambrose of Pylos, dated circa 125 B.C.
The following is the true account of the voyage.

Soon after the ship left, a storm appeared at full gale. The sails tore at the masts of the *Antikythera*, the mighty ship rolling and rising with the treacherous and growing waves as the ship left the cover of a small island. Captain Ambrose of Pylos battled Poseidon himself to keep the ship upright through the deafening groan of failing wood.

"Captain! Should we try the mechanism?" the first mate, Pace of Athens, cried.

Ambrose stared straight into the wall of weather looming over them. Lightning crackled above like a burning wildfire. He pulled the wheel hard to port in an attempt to correct before the next wave, but the swell caught the edge of the hull, and threatened to turn the ship over.

"Use it! And pray to Zeus it works!" Ambrose yelled over the wind.

Pace called to the men to abandon post, and set the mechanism. Some who tried to make it lost their footing and tumbled against the floor, unable to keep upright as the ship rolled slowly. The lucky few who made it pulled a box out from under the net used to secure the mechanism in place. Using the remaining time, they partially lifted the lid of the box.

Suddenly, as by sheer luck, a bolt of lightning changed course, and struck the mechanism with an almighty *bang*, setting the gears within spinning with a white glow. Ambrose closed his eyes as the glow brightened and enveloped the ship and the rough water on his left.

As quickly as it grew the glow diminished until it was a soft shimmer around the clicking gears. Ambrose opened his eyes to see an empty void of black, dotted with a scattered twinkling of stars that formed a band of colour and constellations. The crew looked up in awe at the sight of the Milky Way before them. Very few of them had seen anything like it before.

"Land sighted!" came the call from the crow's-nest.

Ambrose looked up to the top of the mast seeing that, against the night sky, the young boy was not looking toward the horizon, but over the side of the ship. While the rest of the crew admired the sky, the captain made his way slowly to the railing, and looked over. Instead of seeing the sea beneath him…

"It's – it's round," he whispered to himself.

His eyes had fallen upon the deep blue of water, but he could also see the outline of the empire on which they lived turning quickly below him. The outline of Peloponnesus passed by, and disappeared over the curvature of the planet. He saw lands yet uncharted, and waters yet unsailed whizz by as the Earth turned quicker and quicker, night shifting to day, and day into night as quick as an eye blinks. He rushed to alert Pace and the cartographers aboard about what was happening below, but he was unable to do so in time.

Ambrose watched as the men disappeared one by one from the ship, before he saw himself vanish from the *Antikythera*, only to reappear at the helm of an identical ship on calmer waters. The men appeared shaken by the experience, and hid when the original ship fell from the heavens, and shattered on the surface of the water nearby, the mechanism sinking to the bottom in its box.

"We must make haste back to Cape Artemisium!" Ambrose yelled.

The men returned to their posts in a panic, turning the new *Antikythera* around, following their instincts back to the safety of shore. Once the ship was on a steady course, Ambrose stepped down from the helm to his private quarters to focus his mind, attempting to create and memorise a story to tell back on land without mentioning the Gods' Mechanism.

The world's first prototype time machine.

SAMARA ARNOLD

Crescent

"Time 12.00 pm. Temperature 21 degrees."

The words spit out from a discreet hole in the wall. Despite all our technological achievements since entering space, somehow we still haven't managed to make the computer voice sound even remotely human.

My eyes flicker around our small spherical classroom at the twenty other teenagers. They are all wearing their Lunetech glasses while they sit in replicas of old Earth chairs. A red light flickers on my glasses, warning me that if I don't put them back on in ten seconds I will be reprimanded for not doing my work. The problem is that I absolutely hate our current subject – Earth history. It's the same old story about why we live on Crescent.

Crescent is a large sphere-shaped space station that is identical to the moon, and orbits Earth. According to history all humans lived on Earth until 'selfish' people started using up everything we needed to survive. Eventually, the Earth became an uninhabitable wasteland. Meanwhile smart scientists had been building Crescent for the 'good' people that they felt didn't deserve to die. The bad people realised their mistake, and chose to stay behind to fix Earth for us.

One day we will all go back, and live on it together happily ever after. No more space. No more rules. Somehow, though, I don't think it's going to happen. Ever.

The insistent beeping of the glasses interrupts my thoughts. I slowly put them back on, and zone out as I'm shown a video of the old Earth, a never ending stream of horrifying pictures. Then come the pictures of what Earth will be like. A place of happiness filled with smiles and light, with huge areas full of trees. Forests they were called.

The screen fades to black as our daily quota of learning is filled. We line up by the white door like clones, all dressed in the same blue tops and pants. I can't wait to escape from this. Tomorrow is the yearly ceremony where the first-born daughter or son at the age of eighteen can choose to stay on Crescent, or go to Earth. I only remember a handful of people choosing Earth. They were disowned by their families. Yet, I can't stop myself from wanting to go and see it for myself, even if it means never seeing my family again. I want to feel the warmth of the sun on my face, not this harsh artificial lighting. To feel a breeze dance on my skin, not the blast of air-conditioning. Only one more day until my life begins.

Dinner is the next scheduled activity. Any regret I had about leaving my family melts away as the usual conversation happens. My parents start ranting, "You're too unmotivated. Why can't you be more like your sister?" I roll my eyes, and ignore them. Then my sister babbles on about what she learnt today. I try to not look like I want to jump out of an escape hatch. That night as I lie in my bunk unable to sleep because of my sister's snoring, I gaze up at the hologram of the universe on the roof and imagine what it would be like to actually see Earth. Everyone else is probably sound asleep, secure in the knowledge that tomorrow they will pick the thing they've always known – Crescent.

After a restless night of counting stars the day of the ceremony dawns. I drift through it until the sharp instructions jolt me from my reverie. I follow the line of people down the harshly lit corridor. Buzzing surrounds me, yet I feel nothing at all as I robotically enter the large ceremony chamber, and find my space standing at the front. A layer of sweat forms on my hands. My feet tap mutinously. A hush ripples through the room as the captain steps up to the front. His white clothing glows in comparison to our dull colours. The usual scripted speech follows, opening the ceremony.

Then comes the part that everyone is waiting for. The first teenager walks slowly to the front.

He smiles as he states, "I choose Crescent."

He sits down next to his parents. One down, nine more until me. The next person, a girl, also chooses Crescent without any sign of hesitation.

Too quickly it is my turn. I focus on not tripping over as I walk to the front. A battle ensues inside me as I wonder if I really want to leave my home. Then I imagine spending my life here and I am sure of my answer. After a deep breath I stare at the white ceiling, and utter the three small life-changing words, "I choose Earth."

Everyone gapes at me before I am whisked away by a councillor down a maze of featureless walls.

"This is your holding cell. You will be kept here until your passage is arranged." The voice allows no argument.

I am left alone for the first time in forever.

After many hours, I am instructed by the ship's computer to leave the room, and follow the passage until I reach another door. It is dark in the passageway. My fear rises as I try to find the door. Suddenly the ground disappears beneath me. When I next open my eyes, I am in another passage. A wave of nausea washes over me. I quickly close my eyes until it passes.

Ever so slowly, I begin walking through the tunnel. Standing at the end is the captain. The nausea dissipates, replaced by confusion. There is something different about this man.

"Welcome to Earth," he exclaims, as he takes my hand and leads me to a seat.

"E-e-earth," I stutter.

"The reason why I look like your Captain is because I am his double. You have just travelled between two parallel universes. He and I are able to communicate telepathically. Three years ago he warned me what would happen to Earth if we did nothing. Because of that warning, I have managed to prevent what happened in your universe from happening in ours. To show our gratitude we allow access to our Earth, which is why you have been sent here. It stops your ship from being over populated. He is happy, and we are happy."

I slowly absorb all this information. To my surprise I discover that I'm not too bothered by it.

"What do I do now?" I ask.

"Anything," he replies. "You're free."

Free.

The word fills me with hope. Even though this isn't the Earth I knew, I am certain that this is the beginning of a better life.

The Last of Us

"Hello? People of Mars, do you read me?" the woman's voice quavered.

Behind her a young boy, about sixteen, scoffed. She whipped her head around to scowl at him.

"People of Mars…" he sneered.

"Well, what do you want me to call them, wisecrack?" she said, glaring at him.

He stared back for a little while longer before letting out an exasperated sigh. He pushed his dirty blond hair off of his face. Acne was scribbled across his forehead and cheeks.

He looked at the wall to his left, and muttered, "Just hurry it up."

She opened her mouth to argue, but thought better of it, and turned back to the radio.

As she did, a tall man burst through the door, breathing heavily. His eyes darted around the room.

"There's nothing wrong with the satellite." He spoke quickly. "But it's coming. We need to move fast. Keep trying."

The woman held down the button on the transmitter and spoke. "Hello. Earth to Mars. Can you hear this?"

She released her finger, heart pumping in her chest. More static. She shut her eyes and continued to hope.

"We're screwed," the boy said.

She stood up and stormed over to the boy. "If you're not going to say anything useful would you please shut up." He said nothing but raised an eyebrow, which angered her even more. "I can't believe he died for you," she whispered.

The muscles in his neck tensed. "Don't say that. Don't ever say that, damnit!"

He threw a punch that landed on the side of her head. She stumbled, and leant against the wall.

The older man charged forward on two stiff legs. "Knock it off you two!" he said through gritted teeth. "We're trying to survive here. Killing each other is *not* going to help."

The woman narrowed her eyes at the boy.

"You think I don't feel horrible about that?" he breathed. "If it were my choice I wouldn't have let it happen. But it did. It wasn't anyone's decision but his. So just let it go, will you?" He slid down the wall, and tucked up his knees. "I'm sorry that I can't be sorry," he whimpered.

For a moment there was silence. These were the survivors, the ones who had stayed hard as rock, like marble statues. But now there were cracks, and underneath that layer of war, suffering, dirt and ash were patches of light – the one humane thing left of them. It dared to be free again, but the small cracks were all they were going to get. Even if they survived, they would never be able to get rid of what they had become.

The static from the radio seemed to grow louder, hollowing out their insides.

"What are you going to say?" asked the old man.

"Hmm?" The woman snapped out of her daydream.

"What are you going to say happened to all of us? On the radio. If they answer," he explained.

They were all so sure that no one was going to answer, that no one knew what to do if they did.

"At least we can all agree," said the boy. "If anyone is speaking it's you." He pointed towards the woman who gave him a wry smile in return.

The man spoke up again. "Well? What are you going to say, girlie?"

97

She laughed and ran her tongue over her teeth.

"Alright then. What would I say? Three years ago, a nuclear bomb was launched in the northern hemisphere. After the first year, we made the assumption that everyone up north was wiped out, or at least poisoned by radiation. By the third year, the radiation had made its way down south, slowly poisoning everyone. Many people took their own lives not wanting to risk anything. Others wanted to stick it out and try surviving. Most failed. There are three of us in this room. We found this place thanks to a great friend of ours. He helped build it, told us how there was a rocket here, that the co-ordinates were set to your location, and that all we had to do was get you to release it. Without him we would not be here. The Earth sent you people to Mars to help you learn more, but now we need you to help us. Are you still up there? Should we even bother trying to leave if we're just going to die anyway? If we are wrong, please, please report back to us. We don't have much time left, an hour tops. The only way we can leave is if you justify the rocket to launch. Please talk back to us. We're the last of the life forms on this planet. We're the last of us."

The static echoed through the cold room.

"Hello?"

The sudden voice woke the young woman with a start. She rubbed her eyes sleepily and crawled over towards the radio.

"Hello?" repeated the voice. "Is anyone there?"

The woman answered harshly. "You're too late. I'm the last one."

"The last one?"

"Yes, there were three of us, but I managed to give them the last two cyanide pills while they were asleep."

"Cyanide?" the voice on the other end became concerned. "What's going on down there?"

"It doesn't matter now. It's done. Just whatever you do, don't come back to Earth. Ever."

The woman turned away from the radio. The voice was joined by another, both yelling through the speaker. The woman dropped onto all fours, vomiting on the floor. She looked at the two men. She had been travelling with the elder since the start. Her father. He looked at peace, a slight smile on his face. She smiled back at him before turning to look at the boy. He did not look happy, as if you could see all the agony and despair on his face. Poor kid. He never even got to grow up. She didn't even know who he was, only that her husband, the one who had led them to possible safety, had sacrificed his life so that this boy they had never met could live a little longer. She had hated this child for so long, thinking he was the reason her husband had died, that he had killed him. But now she realised. If they had switched places, and the boy had died like he should have, she would not be the one sacrificing herself. She would have had the pill, her husband's orders. He would have had to watch her die.

She thought about all that had happened to the world, and how disgusting some people could be.

This world is ugly, she thought.

But what does that matter now? The cruelness of this world would be no more. She sat back against the cool metal wall, head tilted up towards the ceiling. All she had to do now was wait it out. Wait until the radiation took hold of her. She listened to the voices from a whole other planet.

"Hello?" they urged.

"Is anyone there?"

"Hello?"

LIBBY McCONNELL

Stuck in Space

After the explosion
The galaxy stood still, billions upon billions of light years
away.
We were
stranded
But not apart.

All life was still the very beating heart of the Earth we
knew, frozen in time.
Extra-terrestrials
Lost on Earth but found in the sky.
We had to try.

Blasted by alien guts and all.
The Earth we knew no longer stood tall.
Time stretched on, it seemed.
Intergalactic minutes into hours, hours into days
Yet nothing changed.
A vacuum of sparsity.

Houston had being right all along;
Not that they were much help now.
We were far from Texas, from the Earth we once knew
On the edge of an abyss
About to be killed.
The black hole consuming us like peak hour traffic,
Depositing the mothership at the furthest point of the
galaxy.

Lights flashed on the glass screen
We began soaring upwards
White light shone brightly around
As heaven opened its sky.

This was it.
Was it this?

Metallic gates parted ways like two old friends leaving the
stage,
But the angles looked different in space:
Green scaly skin
Orange blood eyes
We were not in heaven it seemed,
But
one thing was to be deemed

We were far, far, far away
From the Earth we knew,

Stuck in space

That dark frozen day.

The Earth We Knew

"Whiirrrr.

A hovercraft soars high, releasing thick, heavy smoke into the 'sky,'

Once a beautiful, royal blue turned grey.

It's 'for the fuel,' they said. 'For our community,' they said.

A vast sea of floating fish carry on for miles beyond what the eye can see.

Forget vast sea. More like hills.

They put together metal, wires, nuts, and bolts, and behold, the robot came upon us.

"Ooooh!

Aaaah!

First one had it. Then two. Then three. You get the picture.

But wait they never knew this robot needed fuel.

So there! The fish hills grew bigger.

Recycling bins were crushed and incinerated.

The definition of a tree was a plastic blow-up.

The Earth we knew, its beautiful green scenery, the sunrises and sunsets, the beautiful blue sky, all a departed memory.

"That's all for today dear," Granny said, closing the book.

"Do you really think that will happen, Granny?" I found this topic particularly interesting.

"If we try hard enough my dear… try hard *enough*."

Judging Comments

Junior Poetry : *Emma Shi*

First Place: Dying Stars by *Daria Beattie Johnson*

The simple structure of two columns in Daria Beattie Johnson's 'Dying Stars' was aesthetically pleasing from the start and helped bring together the poem as a whole. There were so many highlights throughout this poem, with beautiful lines like "silent beneath dying stars," and amazing description such as "pump of blood in their veins." The imagery of the whisper in the last stanza was simply perfect and made me think about how I definitely wasn't writing poetry this good in year 10! The upbeat tone of the rhyming was perhaps a strange contrast to the raw imagery, but overall, I found myself wondering and thinking of this Earth that Daria so effectively portrayed. It was an excellent piece of writing.

Second Place: Dear Earth by *Nadia Snegirev*

The thing I loved most about Nadia Snegirev's poem was the last stanza. It was such an effective ending, both simple and beautiful, that I was a little heartbroken with all the emotion I was feeling; I found myself missing this broken Earth too. Some great moments in imagery were enough to fulfil this piece. "From our humble beginnings in your heart" was just such a sweet and beautiful line, along with other lines that carried more grandeur such as "To the skyscrapers, the new gods of the sky." The piece was original and lovely to read.

Third Place: Tomorrow by *Harriet Carter*

I liked the experimentation in form in Harriet Carter's 'Tomorrow.' The indented lines placed an emphasis on the words that was really effective in the last stanza. I especially loved the second stanza because it was an absolute delight to read. The imagery of "cinnamon autumns glowed in yesterday's sepia" was absolutely beautiful. Although the poem slips out of this imagery several times it still contained many definite highlights in lines like "peppermint grass," and "indigo skies and sepia autumns." I enjoyed this poem a lot.

Highly Commended: The Earth We Once Knew by *Caitlin Davison*

My highly commended poem for Junior Poetry is Caitlin Davison's 'The Earth We Once Knew.' It was such an enjoyable poem with fun rhymes like "weird things like this" paired with "aliens or machines that go blitz" – a nice addition. A very enjoyable poem.

Senior Poetry: *Emma Shi*

First Place: Stuck in Space by *Libby McConnell*

The moment I started Libby McConnell's poem 'Stuck in Space' I knew the poem that would follow would be something precious. The beautiful imagery throughout tugged at my heart, with phrases like "Lost on Earth but found in the sky." The language was so poignant and delicately placed, and I could tell this writer had thought hard about structure, since each line break created emphasis on the key points in the poem. Overall, it was a poem that was full of delicate imagery and effectively conveyed a tone of longing, making it an easy choice for first place.

Second Place: The Past's Remains by *Justine Lim-Ranola*

Justine Lim-Ranola's 'The Past's Remains' had an enjoyable and consistent tone throughout, which made this poem a pleasure to read. I especially enjoyed this wordplay with lines like "We were the results of / A miscalculation, / That we could survive off / Broken innovations." Along with this, the last stanza was a punchy and effective end that closed off the poem nicely. The precision with which Justine obviously worked on creating this rhythm makes this poem my choice for second place.

Third Place: The Earth We Knew by *Doria Kao*

I was excited to read Doria Kao's 'The Earth We Knew' straight from the start because of the way it was formatted. I love reading poems that experiment with form and so I loved the way in which Doria spaced out the words in speechmarks, giving the impression of voices and whispers all around. I enjoyed the enigmatic imagery of the girl who fit well in the world Doria had crafted. "The earth we cannot call back" was a nice piece of imagery to end the poem on. Other lines such as "A gunshot wounded world" helped bring this poem to life. A nice little piece that deserves third place.

Highly Recommended: The Lurking Shadow by *Laurie Duncan*

Laurie Duncan's 'The Lurking Shadow' is my choice for the Senior Poetry highly commended poem. I highly enjoyed the imagery throughout. One of my favourite lines was "unaware of the hidden eyes." I especially enjoyed the second stanza, where rhythm and structure were very important. The motif of the shadow was a mysterious force in the background and, for the most part, was conveyed effectively.

Junior Prose: *Jan Goldie*

First Place: Route 666 by *Helena Andrews*

A strong beginning throws us into the futuristic setting of Route 666 and right from the start the reader is hooked into a recognizable, almost cinematic setting – the bus on its way to another boring day at school. The difference is, this bus is traversing the desert in a futuristic California.

Helena establishes a strong voice and point of view from the beginning, and the reader is drawn into the setting through Frank's eyes. Backstory details are expertly woven into the story, and the reader is introduced to a host of characters and a harrowing situation seamlessly.

Well thought out use of language and dialogue moves the story forward, picking up pace when the children and the bus face danger. I particularly liked the repetition of the phrase that takes the action to the next level – "She forgot to take the radio." You can almost feel reality sinking in.

I enjoyed the fast pace and action packed scenes towards the end of the piece and loved the final hint of hope.

All in all, a fantastic piece of writing that conjured up a very possible world in a wonderfully cinematic way. Well done!

Second Place: Blind by *Emma Lamb*

Emma Lamb throws the reader straight into a harrowing future Earth – four world wars, the bombing of a continent, the dividing of Europe – and from there, weaves an incredibly interesting new world fraught with strange new realities. Backstory and necessary facts are threaded through the main character's thoughts with ease, and the reader is fed a lot of complicated information in a very clever way. Emma's main character Cäcilie comes across as strong and sensitive, her observations giving us a view of the world shielded by what is obviously a supportive family. However, when Cäcilie comes face to face with the reality of the 'blind camps,' she steps up and faces the horror. Gentle dialogue, wonderful observation and clever language lead us to a wonderfully poignant ending. Great work!

Third Place: Worth This by *Hannah Miller*

A strong feminine lead character grabs our attention in the first line of Hannah Miller's wonderful fantasy story. We're drawn to the anguish in her opening questions – Was it worth this? Was power worth the pain? Was the journey worth the loss? A great start! This intriguing piece of writing succeeds because Hannah is a master of action packed, concise sentences that pick up the pace and keep the reader engaged. The wonderful characters embodying the elements – earth, air, fire, and our narrator, water, are instantly recognisable and used in a unique way. A great piece of writing that left me wanting more!

Highly Recommended: Toxic Roots by *Dana Smagge*

A clever piece of writing that had me asking questions and wanting to know more. Dana offers the reader just enough information to engage in her story without showering us with frivolous details, giving this sombre story a sense of mystery. A strong voice and a one-sided point of view add to the sense that information is missing, hovering on the edge of this tale, and we just have to read between the lines to find it. I loved the way Dana compares the struggle of a dying Earth with her friend's internal struggle. Sad and thoughtful, it left me with a sense of 'what if…' Well done.

Senior Prose: *Jan Goldie*

First Place: The Sun Auction by *Jaynie Yang*

There's a quality to the writing in this piece that I loved right from the start; a kind of 'fly on the wall' feeling that includes the reader in the events about to unfold. We're on a spaceship attending the auctioning off of a piece of the sun. How crazy is that? And yet Jaynie's treatment of her characters puts us at ease straight away. The auction continues as the main characters chat about the situation, life, their experiences, and the fate of Earth, the universe and beyond. Wonderful dialogue, a unique setting and some quirky digs at the past, which accentuate just how far into the future this is, make this a very entertaining read. Jaynie Yang draws the reader in from the beginning, and finishes off with a lovely, well written twist that puts a smile on your face and gives us hope for the future. Fantastic work. Well done!

Second Place: When We Return by *Elysia Harcombe*

Beautiful character development draws the reader into an alien viewpoint, completely immersing us in their world. The fate of Earth is in alien hands – or is that alien tangles? Wonderfully descriptive phrases bring a well-developed backstory to life without hammering us with too many unnecessary details. And yet there is a ton of relevant detail here, and I felt like Elysia really knew her characters incredibly well even before she started writing. I'm sure if I asked her, she'd be able to tell me what they had for dinner the night before! It's that kind of in depth character and world building that makes this story a success. Plus that cliffhanger ending! It left me wanting more. Well done!

Third Place: Crescent by *Samara Arnold*

There's a clarity to Samara's writing that I immediately liked. It has to do with the strong voice of her main character, who I felt empathy with from the first sentence. There's a lovely quirky tone to her observations that brings humour into what is a rather dark situation. She's about to make a life changing decision, and it won't be easy to leave everything behind. I enjoyed the world building, and felt immersed in life as a teenager in space. Plus, the way Samara threaded necessary backstory effortlessly into her main character's thoughts was well handled and well thought out. Great writing. Well done. Keep up the good work!

Highly Recommended: The Cure by *Jacob Jones*

In a futuristic and recognisably kiwi setting, a man holds the cure to a killer disease and he's on the move. Jacob's well-written account of Professor Quill's story is fast paced and action-packed from the start. There's a 'cops and robbers/detective style' feel to this piece that grabbed my attention, and I felt as if Jacob wrote this like a screenplay – it has a cinematic quality. I enjoyed the New Zealand feel to the setting, and this is carried through well with recognisable kiwi dialogue. The action scenes are punchy and well handled. Great work!

Judging Panel:

Emma Shi

Emma Shi was the winner of Senior Poetry for Write Off Line 2013. She was also the winner of the National Schools Poetry Award 2013. Currently, she is studying Classics and English at Victoria University of Wellington.

Jan Goldie

Bay of Plenty based author Jan Goldie's latest creation, Brave's Journey, has just been published by IFWG Publishing Australia. It is a fantasy adventure about a boy called Brave and a girl named True, who travel through a magical world of forests, deserts, strange creatures and ruthless soldiers, going months without a bath as they battle to save their land from the evil ruler, Mallevia. Jan loves coffee, raspberries and champagne so she wouldn't last long on that journey. Find out more at **www.jangoldie.com**.

Cover Art

Kodi Murray

Kodi Murray is a freelance designer/illustrator currently studying for a Bachelor of Media Arts at Wintec. Kodi is just branching into the commercial field where his talents and his passions lie. Building his artistic portfolio, Kodi's work has ranged from commissions for friends, to a commission for a local celebrity, to featuring in The Movie Network [Canada]'s documentary 'Reelside' in 2015.

These and all of Kodi's personal works are viewable online at **www.behance.net/KodiMurrayNZ**.

Editors:

Jean Gilbert

Speculative writer Jean Gilbert moved from Virginia, U.S. to New Zealand in 2005, and has since called the Waikato Valley (the Shire) her home. Jean is a Core member of SpecFicNZ, and is also the coordinator for SpecFicNZ Central. Jean's latest science fiction novels are titled *Shifters* and *Ardus* from the Vault Agency Series published by Rogue House Publishing. You can find her short story *Blonde Obsession* in Baby Teeth: Bite Size Tales of Terror published by Paper Road Press, and *Pride* in Contact Light Anthology. Read more about Jean at **www.jeangilbert.com**, or visit her on Twitter and Facebook.

Chad Dick

Chad Dick, a professional editor and proofreader, lives in Katikati in the Bay of Plenty and works for 100% Proof Ltd (**www.100percentproof.co.nz**). He enjoys assisting others with their writing projects, and loves the positive interactions with authors and writers. In his spare time, he is also a writer of both fiction and non-fiction, and is currently working on a book about global environmental problems.

Project Manager

Piper Mejia

Piper Mejia, an advocate for New Zealand writers and literature, was the co-editor of *Write Off Line* (2012/2013) and *Beyond ...* (2012/2013); collections of writing by New Zealand intermediate and secondary students. She continues to manage both national writing competitions. In 2014 her short story *Lockdown* (included in the horror flash fiction collection *Baby Teeth: Bite-Sized Tales of Terror*) was shortlisted for the Sir Julius Vogel Award for science fiction and fantasy writing, and her young adult novella, *The Fence*, appeared in Conclave: A Collection of Science Fiction and Fantasy. In the same year, she won a national poetry competition for her poem *Sounds of Evolution.* In 2015, her novella *Mika* (co-written with Lee Murray) won the Paper Road Press Shortcuts competition (to be published in the inaugural Shortcuts series in 2015). In her spare time she is a high school English teacher.

www.ingramcontent.com/pod-product-compliance
Lightning Source LLC
Chambersburg PA
CBHW060639130626
46555CB00002B/881